THE *Holly* PROJECT

ANGELA PEARSE

© 2023 by Angela Pearse

The moral right of the author has been asserted.
All rights reserved.
No part of this book may be reproduced or used in any manner without written permission of the copyright owner.
First paperback edition November 2023.
Published by Clamp Ltd. (clamp.pub)

Set in Sabon.
Cover art by My Lan Khuc Valle.

ISBN 978-1-914531-86-6 Paperback (IS)
ISBN 978-1-914531-87-3 Paperback (KDP)

For Chris, who loves snow

Chapter 1

Friday lunchtime, 8 December

I don't own a Christmas jumper, it's against my religion, I type, feeling smug. Excellent, now Andrea from HR won't bother me about it because she'll be too afraid of offending me. But in case she sends a follow-up email to suggest other options, I add: *I'm also against fast fashion, so I went to the charity shops but couldn't find any brightly coloured jumpers (or ones with sparkly wool either). They must've already been snapped up by the students!*

It's like clockwork. Every December, the casual but firm request comes through that everyone wear Christmas jumpers on Zoom calls. UGH. I hate this time of year. If it were up to me, I'd take the whole month off and go somewhere that doesn't celebrate it, like Outer Mongolia. But I'm at the business end of a project, so I can't. I'll just have to grit my teeth and power through.

A low growl emits from underneath the desk. Crumpet, my mini schnauzer, is picking up on my black mood. He's my emotional support pet, and we're so in tune that sometimes I think he's me in fur form.

'Exactly,' I tell him, nudging his flank with my foot. 'Buckle up. We're entering festive hell, and it's going to be a bumpy ride.'

I'm well aware that my reluctance to join in on the office cheer will be noted by upper management. But why should I have to wear a silly jumper if I don't want to?

I grab Crumpet's lead, and he bounds around, mad with joy. This dog loves going outside, unlike me. I work from home, so there's no commute and no annoying colleagues chatting in my ear. Ordering groceries online means no queuing at the checkout or shopper drama either. The only reason I leave the house these days is to walk Crumpet. Bliss.

On the street, the frigid air that fills my lungs is a shock to the system after the warmth of my second-floor flat. It's so cold I can feel icicles forming on my nostril hairs.

'Maybe just a quick walkie,' I say to Crumpet, burrowing deeper into my scarf. At this time of year it's dark at 3 p.m. and I don't want to be outside for longer than I have to. Crumpet doesn't need telling twice; he's already straining against his lead, eager to get going.

I live a couple of streets over from the Royal Mile, but we head in the opposite direction, away from the holidaymaker hoo-ha. There's no way I'm getting involved in that throng of commercialism. No, we're heading to the local graveyard, where the people are much less lively and it's wonderfully quiet.

Creaking open the black wrought-iron gate, we slip through and walk amongst the avenues of mossy graves interspersed with dripping wet boughs. Relief. This is my small pocket of peace in the middle of busy Edinburgh. Even Crumpet stills for a moment, and I bend to let him off his lead. He likes snuffling around the crumbling headstones, and occasionally, there's the odd mouse to chase.

Propping myself up against a sturdy rectangular crypt with a praying angel, I check my phone for messages. Four calls gone to voicemail. The first three are easily dealt with: the mother, the father, Violet—delete, delete, delete. The fourth is unexpected. It's from Lewis Kirkcaldy, the CEO of the hotel we're currently working with to implement sustainability measures. He never calls me. What does he want? Hopefully, it's nothing bad. The project is going well from my perspective. With some trepidation, I play the message.

'Hi, Holly. It's Lewis. Just a brief end-of-week call to say good job on setting up the third stage of the initiative. Looks like we're on track, but there's an addition I'd like to discuss with you. I'll send through a Google invite for a Zoom early next week. Have a good weekend ... Oh, by the way, you're all invited to our Christmas party on Friday, the 22nd, at the hotel. I've emailed the details to Andrea.'

I lean back on the crypt and heave a deep sigh. There's no way I'm going to that! I'll have to come up with some excuse. Lewis's hotel is high-end. I'm sure he'll pull out all the stops to make it a great party, but the thought of having to endure drunken conversations with people—and at Christmas, no less—makes my skin crawl.

However, it would be interesting to meet Lewis face to face. We've had dozens of Zoom calls, but he never has his webcam on and just uses audio. He said something about it being broken, which I might believe. But I checked him out on LinkedIn, and there's no photo on there either. I'm intrigued, but not enough to go to his Christmas party.

I whistle to Crumpet, who's busily nosing about through a pile of dead leaves. But he ignores me as usual. 'Come on, mate! It's freezing.' I'm just about to go over and fetch him when there are heavy footsteps on the path.

'Excuse me. Is that your dog?' I turn to see an older woman rugged up in a tweed coat and a fawn scarf, her brown stockinged legs tapering into a pair of sensible brogues of the same colour. She stops alongside me and peers through her wire-rimmed glasses at Crumpet, who's now sniffing at a headstone.

'Yes,' I say, expecting a formulaic 'Och, sooooo cute'.

But it's not forthcoming.

Instead, I get 'This is sacred ground. It's not a dog park', said in a hoity-toity manner, which instantly gets my back up.

'I've been coming here for months, and no one's ever said anything.' In fact, I've never seen a soul, and how dare she assume I'm not visiting some dearly departed relative that left this earth in 1885!

'Well, they should. I've half a mind to report you to the council.'

'By the time they look into it, we might both be six feet under ourselves,' I say, attempting to make a joke.

But she just eyes me sternly without cracking a smile. She obviously doesn't get my sense of humour, or she works for the council. A phone is pulled out of her pocket. 'What's your name?'

I roll my eyes. 'It's Ms We're Just Leaving. Crumpet, come here!' I call.

He runs over, and the woman watches as I fasten his lead.

'See, no harm done. No graves desecrated,' I say sarcastically.

'You've got a right mouth on you.'

Sensing this exchange is about to get heated, Crumpet lifts his leg, and a stream of yellow urine soaks the woman's stockings and runs down onto her shoe. Her mouth drops open. 'He did that on purpose!' she screeches angrily.

'He didn't. He just thought your leg was a tree trunk.'

'Ooooot! Get oooot, the both of you! Dirty dooooog!' She flaps her hands at me like she's swatting flies.

I scoop him up and make haste towards the gate, leaving the crazy woman to it. I'm having a quiet chuckle to myself when we're out of earshot, then realise Crumpet's gurgling in my arms, like he's laughing too.

Back at my flat, the run-in with the woman has put me in a weird mood. I have all this enraged energy and no outlet for it. It's not a good idea, but I do it anyway. I ring the family. I know why they're all calling at the same time. It's the 'coerce Holly down to London for Christmas' campaign. They should space out the calls so I don't get suspicious. The mother first. She's the easiest to deal with, though she tends to be good at emotional blackmail.

Sure enough, after five minutes of meaningless chit-chat, 'Holly, it was your grandmother's eightieth birthday this year,' she wheedles. 'She's had pneumonia, gallstones, and Covid. I doubt she's going to be around another year. We're visiting her at the rest home in Battersea since this might be her last Christmas.'

'Sounds like she's done all right so far. She'll probably outlive you all,' I say, checking the fridge to see what I can cook for tea. 'And please don't say "last Christmas"—I don't want that Wham! song stuck in my head.'

The father comes on and goes one better, saying that *he's* the one on his last legs and it'll be lucky if he makes it to New Year's Eve. 'At least you'll go out with a bang,' I tell him, turning on the grill. I was thinking of cooking some tofu because the hotel's environmental changes have inspired me and I'm trying to eat more plant-based food. But let's face it—I need sustenance after talking to the parents ... Sausages it is.

Next up, I call my sister, Violet, who goes straight for the jugular as soon as I decline her invitation too. 'You're a sad, pathetic loser for wanting to spend Christmas by yourself.'

'Well, maybe I won't be alone. I might be spending it with friends.'

'You don't have any friends,' she scoffs.

She's right, but I'm not going to admit that.

'I do too. Her name's Lila. She's an ex-client, and she lives in Inverkeithing.' Huh, it actually sounds plausible. But Violet isn't buying it.

'Lila equals big, fat lie.'

After hanging up, I feel soul drained. Honestly, I don't know why they want me to go down to London for Christmas so much. They never bother with me for the rest of the year. And it's never a good time hanging out with them—the family are not fun people. Besides, I'm actually looking forward to sleeping in and catching up on Netflix. Maybe I'll eat sausages for breakfast, lunch, and dinner too. Now there's a thought, and I know Crumpet will be on board.

First thing Monday morning, Andrea asks if I'm available for an urgent Zoom. I steel myself for a gentle but firm bollocking. There's a reason she's in HR: she's good at getting people to follow the rules.

'If this is about the jumper thing, I really don't have one.'

'It's not about that,' she says, leaning forward and tilting her laptop screen so she's in full view.

Andrea has straight dark hair like me, but whereas mine is long and nondescript, hers is styled in a jaunty chin-length bob. I wonder where she gets it cut. We're friendly enough, but it feels a bit personal to ask.

'I wanted to talk to you about something else. Lewis Kirkcaldy has invited the whole team to their Christmas party at the hotel. He sent me through the details on Friday.'

'Yeah, I know. He left a message on my phone and mentioned something about it.'

'So are you going?'

'Uh, probably not. I don't do parties.' I could attempt to

make up an excuse, but she knows me well enough by now.

Andrea looks at me silently for a few seconds, as if she's trying to gauge how I'll react to what she's about to say.

'I really think you need to in this case.' I detect a faint note of concern in her tone. That gets my attention.

'Why? What's going on?'

'It was just something Melanie overheard Valerie saying on the phone, which is probably nothing ...' Valerie is my line manager; and in my experience, when she says something to anyone, it's usually *not* nothing. Andrea is good friends with Valerie's PA, Melanie, who has proven herself to be a reliable source of information.

Andrea bites her lip and shifts uncomfortably. 'It may not be about you.'

'You may as well tell me.'

'She said that certain key team members need to start being more *present*. It was fine during Covid, as we were all adjusting to working from home. But now that things are back to normal, there needs to be more visibility and social involvement.'

Huh, that's kind of rich, especially since Lewis Kirkcaldy never shows his face on Zoom. At least I turn my camera on.

'I just thought I should warn you,' Andrea continues. 'I'm sure she wasn't meaning you specifically, but you might want to put in an appearance just to keep her off your back. After all, you are the project manager. It will look a bit weird if you're not there. Besides, it's a Christmas party! It'll be fun—'

I cut her off before she starts waxing lyrical about the joys of the season. 'OK, thanks for the heads-up.'

'So I can mark you down as going?' she says brightly.

'Fine,' I mutter.

I spend the rest of the morning fuming, feeling like a trapped rat at having to go to the stupid Christmas function. Parties are so *not* in my wheelhouse, especially Christmas parties. I don't like being coerced into something 'just in case'. But I do like this job. I don't want to be laid off for something menial like not being more visible. I'm not even sure you can fire someone for that. But I suppose I could be managed out. Next thing I could be on a PIP and having to prove my worth.

Crumpet whines from underneath the desk.

'I know how you feel, mate. Festive hell just took a turn for the worse.'

Chapter 2

Friday evening, 22 December

I'm jammed into a lift with a bunch of women in gaudy outfits chattering at high decibels. The one in front of me is wearing a purple sequin dress and a reindeer headband. She's shorter; and every time, she moves, Rudolph's antlers smack me in the face. This is *not* how I choose to spend my time. I close my eyes, rub my temple, and take a deep breath.

I was praying this Christmas do was going to be a sedate affair of sipping mulled wine, lounging on comfy sofas, and engaging in pleasant conversation. But I've got a bad feeling it's going to be a 'screeching to be heard over unsk unsk music' one. Luckily, I'll only be here for fifteen minutes. Max.

The lift doors open, and we all spill out onto a highly polished marble floor that's slippery as fuck. I'm fine because I'm wearing black rubber-soled combat boots, so I adjust my matching black minidress and march off towards the faint sound of music, leaving the women to clutch at one another and gasp in their spindly heels. Not my problem.

Upon entering the function room, I'm pleasantly surprised. I was expecting to be assaulted with cheesy Christmas tunes, but there's a string quartet set up in the corner playing an uplifting rendition of Beyoncé's 'Single Ladies'. The room is half full of people, and not everyone is wearing sequins, thank God.

'Holly! You made it.' Andrea breaks off from a nearby huddle and greets me with a big grin.

'Well, it was either that or get fired,' I say grumpily.

But she doesn't react, just smiles, and runs her eye over my outfit. 'Nice dress. I like the batwing sleeves.'

'Thanks.'

'Where did you get it from?'

'The back of my wardrobe.'

Andrea laughs, but I'm not joking. I went digging last night to find something to wear and discovered a whole bunch of clothes stuffed in there from ten years ago, when I used to be marginally more fun. I've also run out of contact lenses, so I'm wearing oversized glasses with black chunky frames. The whole ensemble is making me look like a nerd attending a funeral rather than a Christmas party. Whatever.

I push my glasses back up my nose and scan the room.

'So which one is the famous Mr Kirkcaldy?' All I need to do is give him is a quick hello and a handshake so Valerie is satisfied I'm being more *visible*. Then I can get the hell out.

'I don't think he's here yet. It's an open bar, so I'll get some drinks. Why don't we sit over there?' She nods to a row of unoccupied buttery-suede couches alongside a ten-foot-high window looking out over the city. Everyone's chatting in groups, and I can't see anyone else from my team, so I'm relieved Andrea seems to want to hang out. Otherwise, I'd be standing in the corner like Nancy No-Mates.

'OK.' I head over and settle in, and she comes back with two tumblers of what I think is Coke until I take a sip. It's got enough rum in there to strip paint. I pull a face.

'Is it all right? He was a bit heavy-handed.'

'It's fine. I need it.' I take a longer swallow, and the alcohol makes my ears tingle. Andrea sits opposite me and crosses her legs. She's wearing a cornflower-blue pencil skirt with a black skivvy and looks like she's come straight from the office.

'It's great you came, I know you hate parties,' she says. I feel a rush of relief and companionship that she understands.

'Yeah. One drink and I'm out of here.'

'Oh, stay and keep me company for a couple at least. We

haven't clapped eyes on Lewis yet.'

I sigh and scan the milling crowd. The party appears to be gathering momentum, and the string quartet has changed it up a notch to Bon Jovi's 'Livin' on a Prayer'. 'I don't even know what he looks like,' I say idly.

'I do.'

'Wait, what? How do you know? He said his webcam was broken!'

Andrea laughs. 'I haven't seen him on Zoom, but he is on TikTok.'

'Seriously?'

She nods. 'Oh yes, he's quite active on there. He does these great foodie vids, where he visits different restaurants in Edinburgh. They're quite entertaining.'

I can't see why it would be. 'So does he just film his plate with a caption or what?'

'No, it's more interactive than that. There are a few where he's talking to the camera and giving his opinion, like a live food critic. The latest one was really funny. It had lots of comments.'

OK, that's got me curious. 'What's his profile name?'

'Eating Local with Lewis? Something like that.' She pulls her phone from her handbag, and I notice we're both down to the dregs of our rum and Cokes.

'Do you want another drink?'

'Definitely. I'll find the vid and send it through to you.'

While she fiddles with her phone, looking for the TikTok, I head over to the oval-shaped bar, where the partygoers are corralling the barman and getting top-ups. This could take a while.

I'm staring intently at my phone, waiting for Andrea to send through the video so I can get a heads-up on Lewis, when a male voice drawls lazily, 'Are you hoping someone will call you?'

'Huh? No,' I reply distractedly, keeping my eyes on my phone. *Go away now please.*

'So you're going to call them?'

He seems insistent on talking to me, so I sigh and give him some attention. He's around mid-thirties with medium-length dark hair slicked back from a broad forehead, an aquiline nose, and a chin dimple. He's wearing a dark suit with a white shirt. Good-looking in a sharkish kind of way.

'No,' I say brusquely. 'I'm waiting to get a drink.'

A man brushes past with a pint of beer in one hand and claps the guy on the shoulder with the other. 'Great party, Lewis!'

I stare at him, taken aback.

'*You're* Lewis?'

He nods and says, 'Aye, Lewis Kirkcaldy.' Then he holds out his hand for me to shake, which I do, limply. Thank

God I wasn't actively looking at his TikTok. His voice sounds different in real life, and he doesn't match the picture I'd formed in my head, so I'm having to make some mental readjustments.

'Nice to finally meet you in the flesh, Holly.'

'Er, likewise.' My phone beeps, and I quickly turn off the ringer. That'll be the TikTok.

'I think we can move this queue along, don't you?' he says, gazing at the crowd. 'We'll be here all night otherwise.'

With the practised air of someone who's used to commanding people to do what he says, Lewis efficiently clears a path for us through to the front of the bar.

'What are you having?'

My mind goes blank. 'I can't remember.'

Lewis chuckles. 'I have that effect on people.'

'Hah. Two rum and Cokes please.'

He raises an eyebrow.

'They're not both for me,' I assert. 'One's for Andrea.'

'Ah, the lovely steel-wooled Andrea.' He slaps his cheek smartly. 'Sorry, did I say "wooled"? I meant steel-*willed*. I've had a few.'

I laugh at that. 'She does have a firm hand. You probably need it, though.'

Oooh, am I flirting? I have been binge-watching *The Witcher*, and Lewis does have a Henry Cavill chin.

Luckily, he doesn't seem to notice and slouches against the bar—his bar, I guess, since he runs the place. He swings into business mode.

'Thanks again for accommodating that last-minute addition. The recycled bottle duvet is an important part of our guilt-free sleep marketing campaign.' He shrugs. 'Who knew you could even make duvets out of plastic bottles?'

'I know, this sustainability project has certainly been eye-opening for me too. I've started buying tofu to save the planet,' I say.

He cocks an eyebrow. 'Ah, but are you eating it?'

'Well, no,' I admit with a guilty smile. 'It's in my fridge. I just have to find the right recipe.'

Too late, I remember Lewis is a foodie, and he probably knows twenty delicious ways to cook tofu.

But he just grins and says, 'Check out Olive. That's a good recipe site.'

He hands me the rum and Cokes, and I sip one. It tastes even stronger than before.

'Where are you sitting?'

'I'm over there with Andrea.' I nod at the couches where Andrea is talking to some guy wearing a red Christmas jumper and black trousers.

'Looks like Bailey's keeping her company.'

'Who's he?'

'One of my friends who's rather into the festive season, as you can see.'

As we get closer, I note that his friend Bailey also has a flashing bow tie and is wearing elf ears.

Good lord, he's a walking Christmas cliché. I'm instantly repulsed.

Andrea looks up as we approach. 'Oh, there you are, Holly. I see you ran into Lewis.'

'I did.' I hand her a rum and Coke and pointedly don't look at Bailey, who I'm sure is dying for me to notice him in his tacky get-up.

'Hi, Lewis.' Andrea gives me a knowing look, which I return. *Yes, I'm going to be all over that TikTok as soon as I'm alone.*

'Andrea—mind if I sit here?' he asks.

'Of course not.' She shifts over, and Lewis sits down next to her, and they start talking about something to do with the project.

I sense Bailey checking me out from his position opposite them on the couch. Sigh. I really don't want to talk to him, but sure enough, he clears his throat. 'Hi, I'm Bailey.'

'Holly,' I mutter.

'Are you a client of Lewis's?'

'Yes, I've been managing his sustainability project.'

'Oh, cool.'

I glance at him while he's taking a sip of his drink. He's got a sweep of golden-brown hair, brown eyes, round cheeks with dimples, and underneath the latex, I assume, normal-sized ears. He does make a cute elf, I have to admit. But his bow tie is flashing so rapidly and brightly I feel the pinprick of a headache starting behind my left eyeball. He sees me staring at him.

'Sorry, do you want to sit down?'

'No, I'm fine.'

He frowns. 'You do know this is a Christmas party?'

'I'm well aware,' I say dryly.

He nods at my dress. 'You need a bit of colour then.'

Before I know what's happening, Bailey pulls something out of a tote bag, stands up, and plonks a Santa hat on my head. 'That's better. You can keep it. I've got spares.'

I yank the hat off and throw it at him. 'No thanks!'

'Leave her alone, Bailey. Not everyone's into dressing up like you,' interjects Lewis from the sidelines.

Bailey bends down to pick the Santa hat from off the floor, his face crimson. I feel a little disconcerted that he's not saying anything. But his Santa hat move was pushy, and why is he so into Christmas?

Thank God I never have to see him again to find out.

Chapter 3

Lewis leans in closer. 'So you've told me all the ice cream flavours you don't like. Which ones *do* you like?'

We're on our fourth round of drinks, and the rum is starting to work its magic. My head feels distinctly floaty and disconnected from my body. The string quartet has been replaced by a DJ, the lights have been lowered, and there's a mishmash of people dancing. Bailey is out on the floor with Andrea, who's wearing the Santa hat. His bow tie flashes merrily as he does some kind of jerking robot move. Just seeing him annoys me.

I try to focus on Lewis's face, which is starting to roll sideways. 'I like Ben & Jerry's Pish ... Pish ... Oh no, I can't say it.' I lightly bump Lewis's shoulder. 'You try.'

'Pish ... Phish Food,' he manages. 'God, you've got me going now.'

'I think I *am* pished. I was meant to leave an hour ago.'

He smirks. 'Isn't this better than an early night and a cup of Horlicks?'

I look away, slightly offended. He's obviously pinned me as some kind of loser. 'I'm just not a party person. I should go,' I mumble, reaching for my purse.

He pats my shoulder lightly and peers into my face. 'Hey, I'm just teasing. You're fun to talk to. Stay for a bit longer.'

'OK. Just for a bit, though,' I counter. Bailey is now bobbing up and down and it's making me feel tired just watching him.

So I take it you're not a fan of elves?' Lewis says slyly when he sees me staring at Bailey. I quickly look away. 'Yeah, I had a run-in with a perverted elf when I was a kid,' I remark before I know what I'm saying.

Lewis snorts but stops laughing when he sees I'm serious. I don't elaborate on that. 'Er, let's just say Christmas isn't my favourite time of year. I find the commercialism nauseating.'

'I get that, but it's also a chance to RR&R—reconnect with family, relax, and refocus,' he says. 'And presents don't have to be expensive. It's the thought that counts.'

I sense Lewis is one of those curious, bordering-on-nosey people who, once they get a whiff of mystery, keep digging until they find out the raw truth. I just shrug. I'm not about to spill my life story to a willing ear at a Christmas party.

The DJ turns up the volume, and I wince at the noise.

'Why don't we go somewhere quieter? Have a nightcap,' Lewis suggests.

I'm instantly suspicious. 'Where?'

'My suite.'

I'm impressed despite myself. 'You have a suite?'

'My father owns the hotel—of course I have a suite. Come on, it's getting hard to hear ourselves think out here. And I want to show you the recycled bottle duvet.'

'Sounds remarkably like you want to show me your etchings.'

Lewis holds up his hands. 'There's nothing dodgy in it, I promise. I have a girlfriend.'

'Where is she?'

'In Brussels. She works for the EU.'

How convenient. But the noise *is* deafening, and I am a bit curious about the suite and the duvet.

'Fine. Then I really do have to go.'

'Of course.'

Lewis's suite is two floors down, a plush corner room in muted tones boasting a super king-sized bed and a separate lounge area with an impressive Art Deco sideboard. There are two bendy metal floor lamps with glowing gold shades lighting the space and a peek of the castle out the window.

'Nice decor,' I say, leaning against the doorframe. Although my senses are dumbed by rum, I still have the presence of mind to wonder if fraternising with a client is a good idea.

'Come in. Don't loiter by the door,' he says, waving me

over to the bed. 'Check this out.'

Oh yes, the famous duvet. Unsteadily, I launch off from the doorframe like a ship from port, and the door swings closed with a click. Decision made. Too late now.

'Feel it, you'd never know the difference.' Lewis holds out the edge of the peacock-blue duvet cover to me.

I squish it in my fist like a marshmallow. 'It's so soft!'

Lewis beams. 'More than three million water bottles are going to be diverted from landfill into the hotel's bedding.'

'That's great.'

'I know, it feels really good to be doing something to clean up the planet.'

'I bet.'

But I'm not sure I could sleep under this duvet, knowing people's mouths have been on the bottles that it was made from. Euch. But I don't tell him that.

'Do you live here?' I enquire as we make our way to the lounge area. Lewis waves me to a comfy-looking green velvet armchair, and he sits opposite me on a fawn leather couch, a polished dark-wood coffee table between us.

'No, I just use the room when I come here for functions,' he says. 'I live in Leith.'

'With your girlfriend?'

'Yes, though Moira's away so much, and I'm busy here. We're like ships that pass in the night. But she said she'd try to make it to the party later.'

'Cool.'

'Anyway, enough about me. Tell me more about you.'

'I'm not that interesting.'

His lips curl, showing the tips of even white teeth. 'I beg to differ.'

I readjust my glasses on my nose and don't say anything.

'Why don't we play a game? If I guess something right about you, you have to down a shot of tequila. And vice versa.'

Since I like games I can win, I agree. There's no way he's going to guess my secrets.

'OK. Where's the tequila?'

'Voilà!' Lewis presses the corner of the sideboard behind the couch, and the door springs open to reveal a sizeable spirit collection, including at least a dozen bottles of whisky.

I goggle at the selection. 'Wow, that's a lot of whisky.'

'Bailey's parents live in Speyside,' he explains. 'When we go up there, his dad likes taking us round the distilleries.'

Irritation sparks at the mention of Bailey. I don't know why I've got such a thing against him. But I'm like that with people sometimes—I just dislike them immediately. Lewis seems cool, though.

A couple of shot glasses appear, and he pours clear liquid from a slender bottle. 'I'll go first.' He taps his finger against his Cavill chin and surveys me thoughtfully. 'You're an only child.'

'Errrr, wrong.' Well, Violet technically is my sister.

'Shit. I was sure about that. Your turn.'

I take a stab in the dark. 'You're an *X-Men* fan.'

'Nope. Can't stand those movies.' He eyes his tequila shot like he really wants to drink it.

He tries again. 'You're not on any social media platforms.'

'Huh, I'm not actually. How did you know that?'

'I checked because I was going to follow you and ... nada.'

'I'm not sure that counts. It's prior knowledge.'

'It still counts. Drink up!'

I toss back the shot, and it slides down my throat like burning citrus, making me gasp.

Lewis refills my glass. 'Why not, by the way?'

'Social media? Because it's toxic and brain destroying. I'd rather read a book. And while we're on the subject, what's with not showing your face on Zoom?'

'I don't want my employees to be fazed by my looks,' he says seriously, and I choke back a laugh. Oh, the arrogance. He nods at his glass. 'Your turn.'

I've got to get one right. Well, if prior knowledge is allowed ...

'You're a foodie, and you like eating out at restaurants.'

'Correct. A lucky guess.' He narrows his eyes at me.

I silently congratulate myself as Lewis downs his shot. I'm so going to nail this game.

Chapter 4

The next morning

I crack open an eye and slam it shut again as light filters through. Ow, that hurt. My brain starts sputtering to life like an old car. Ugh, I feel like shit. My mouth is so dry I can barely swallow. Something weird is also going on with my head. It feels constricted. Gingerly, I reach up and touch something crinkly. Tugging it off, I stare at the object in my hand. Why the hell am I wearing a shower cap? And why am I lying in bed fully dressed?

With an effort, I try to remember ... then see through blurry eyes the peacock duvet and the lounge area. Oh my god, I'm still at the hotel. Lewis! I swivel my head too fast, and a stabbing pain makes me yelp. The other side of the bed is empty and unslept in. OK, it must've gotten too late for me to go home; and I stayed the night, underneath the recycled bottle duvet ... No big deal. There's no evidence of anything untoward happening. Or that Lewis even stayed here with me. I'm not naked. It's all fine.

Groggily, I reach for my phone, but it's not on the nightstand. Instead, there's my glasses, which I put on, and a tumbler of water, which I chug down thankfully, still trying to piece together the events of last night. But they elude me, like someone's dangling a prism in the sun and I'm attempting to snatch at dancing rainbows.

I get out of bed and discover I'm barefoot. Someone (me?) took off my boots, but they're nowhere to be seen. Hobbling over to the lounge area, I spy my phone lying on the coffee table next to a nearly empty bottle of tequila and two upturned shot glasses. The scene of the crime. I creep back to bed, softly and hunched over, so I don't make any jarring movements. Somehow, I think I'm better off being horizontal than upright. But when I'm back under the duvet and fully stretched out, my foot hits something hard. Reaching down a hand, I draw up a black object by its cord. A hairdryer? Why is there a hairdryer in the bed?

Something is off with all this. An eco-friendly shower cap and a hairdryer does not bode well.

My phone displays a bunch of missed calls from Andrea, which ceased just before midnight. Either she gave up, or she got lucky. I really hope she didn't get together with that guy Bailey. We were well on the way to becoming friends, and if *he's* around, that's a no go.

I gaze at the shower cap and the hairdryer lying next to

me on the bed, feeling uneasy. Then I look at my phone again. It's just gone 9 a.m. If I was that drunk, why hasn't Lewis messaged to check up on me? Unless he's crashed out at his flat in a tequila-induced coma. A wave of nausea hits me even though I'm lying down. Then it occurs to me. Oh no, Crumpet! He's probably wondering where I am—starving hungry and, if I'm really unlucky, pooping all over the carpet. I need to get out of here and see to him. If I can find my boots, that is …

After finding my boots placed side by side in the wardrobe, I attempt to make myself look presentable and slouch back to my flat, feeling like I'm doing the walk of shame. Crumpet is beside himself with joy that I've materialised.

'Sorry, buddy, last night was a write-off. We'll go for a walk shortly.' *If I don't power chuck first.* I feed him and nibble tentatively on a piece of dry toast to see how my stomach holds it. I can't even look at the butter, and jam is out of the question.

I can't remember the last time I was this hungover. Actually, I don't think I ever have been—not even in my wild, misspent youth. A vision of Lewis laughing and me yelling 'Pour, pour!' vaguely swims into my mind, and I cringe. God, he must've guessed right quite a few times for me to have drunk so many shots. Hopefully, I was just drinking for the sake of it and not incriminating myself in any way. There's something, though, a memory lying just below the surface that I can't quite grasp.

Did we? Surely not. I would've remembered that! Besides, I was fully dressed when I woke up. *You can still have sex with someone while wearing clothes, don't be naive*, a little voice whispers. With that thought, I hotfoot it to the bathroom, strip, and inspect my lower region fully. But there's no dried semen. Nothing feels sore, and I just don't think it happened. But I feel scared all the same, like he's violated me in some way. *You fucking idiot, Holly! Why the fuck did you go to his hotel room?*

After showering, washing my hair, and drinking a litre of water, I feel marginally better. My phone lights up on the bed; Andrea again. I answer with a curt, 'Hello.'

'Holly! Thank fuck! I rang you so many times last night. Why didn't you pick up? I thought you were dead!' She sounds so relieved to the point of tears that I soften.

'I know, I should've called you back first thing. Sorry. I'm not dead. I just had a bit too much to drink. I'm at home now.'

'You spent the night at the hotel?'

'Uh ... yes.'

'Were you with someone?'

I gulp. 'Yes.' *Maybe best to change the subject.*

'What about you? What time did you leave?' I enquire.

'Around eleven. The party was just getting started. I wasn't sure where you were, so I called. But then you didn't pick up, and I got worried. Lewis came in just as I was leaving.'

I blink at that. 'Did he mention me?'

'No, I asked him if he'd seen you, and he said he hadn't. That's why I tried calling you again.'

'But I was with him!'

'With Lewis?' Andrea sounds confused. 'You spent the night in Lewis's hotel room?'

'Yes! I may have had a bit too much to drink, and he kindly let me use his bed.'

Andrea doesn't say anything. The uneasy vibe I had when I woke up intensifies. Something fishy is going on with this guy.

'Hello ...? Andrea?' I say, worried that she's going to think I'm some kind of slag who sleeps with clients. 'I should clarify he wasn't in the bed too! Nothing happened with him. It wasn't like that.'

'I'm here. I believe you. I was just checking something,' she replies.

Phew, the relief I feel is palpable. I need Andrea on my side, and not just for HR purposes.

When she speaks again, her voice is calm. But there's an

underlying seriousness to it, like when a policewoman is delivering bad news. 'Holly, I don't want to freak you out. But Lewis posted something involving you on TikTok last night. I'll send it through.' She doesn't say what it's about, just adds using that same calm voice, 'I'm going to watch it all now. Call me back when you've seen it.'

The 'watch it all' bit of her sentence has me curious. What exactly has he posted? A sweeping room shot where you can see my head in the background? Some kind of climate change promo tagging me in it?

My expectation levels are low. So I get a fright when I see a close-up of my pale face, sans glasses, staring at the camera with an eye-piercing scowl. Lewis's voice sounds from off camera like a radio announcer, 'My mate Holly has a Christmas message for you all ... Take it away, Holly.'

My scowl deepens, and my lip curls. 'Yeah, so listen up, TikTokers ...'

What follows is a rant about the evils of consumerism and how Christmas is nothing but Western capitalist propaganda designed to extract money from our wallets.

I breathe deeply. Dear God. Did I really say that? It's what I think, but I normally keep my opinions to myself.

But it's not over yet. The scene changes to me perched on the edge of the bed. There's obviously been a lot more tequila shots happening off camera. My mascara has smudged into two dark circles under my eyes; and I'm wearing, of all things, an eco-friendly shower cap and holding a hairdryer like it's a microphone. The pieces of the puzzle start falling into place.

My anti-Christmas rant continues, and I'm angry-slurring every second word. 'Santa is an asshole, and his elves are worse. Tiny tinkering fools, tap tap tapping with their hammers, making boring shit that no one wants.' Then I start on the reindeers, the carols, and all the other elements that make up the festive hell I'm forced to endure each year. My loathing of eggnog even gets a mention. Cringing, I force myself to watch to the bitter end.

'And anosher thing ...' I pause, as if I'm trying to think of something meaningful to say, but all that comes out is 'Have a crappy Christmas'. I flick two middle fingers up smartly, then collapse backwards onto the bed—and start snoring. A gentle rendition of 'Jingle Bells' starts playing, and the camera switches to Lewis's smirking face. He holds a finger to his lips, whispers 'shhhh', and winks. The video cuts off.

The TikTok has over 500,000 views, 43,500 likes, and 1,500 comments. The back of my neck starts sweating. Feeling sick to my stomach, I click to read the comments but then wish I hadn't.

U crack me up Lewis, this is hilarious. Sharing right now!

This is the funniest thing ever. UNJOLLY HOLLY.

Omg she needs serious help.

A real life grinch! Where did u find her?

*Is she acting? So f***ing funny.*

What a bitch, Santa is cool.

I like her dress but she needs a decent haircut.

And on and on. I scroll through an endless debate. The comments are falling into three main camps: people that think I'm mean and awful, people that agree with me wholeheartedly, and people that have an opinion about my hair, make-up, or clothes. There are a small but growing number who are confused about why I'm wearing a shower cap—I'd like to know that myself.

The TikTok clocks up another thousand views just while I'm looking at it. The thing has a life of its own. I chuck my phone away like it's electric, and it thumps screen down on the carpet. TikTok is crucifying me—two days before Jesus's birth. There's some irony in that, but right now, I can't see the funny side.

This hangover isn't helping. I have heart palpitations and

blurry vision. I crawl over to the phone and quickly text Lewis, *This is Holly. I saw the TikTok please delete it NOW!*

I wait with bated breath for a full five minutes. Please please please reply! But there's nothing. Either he hasn't gotten my text, or he has and is ignoring me. I dial his number. It goes straight to an out-of-office voicemail: 'Hi, I'm on holiday until 28 December. But leave a message if it's urgent, and I'll get back to you then. Merry Christmas!'

Upon hearing his smarmy, upbeat tone, my anger threatens to erupt. But I try to keep a lid on it. My message is curt and to the point: 'Lewis, Holly. The TikTok you posted of me is going viral. I can't believe you did that without my consent. I'm going to report it now, and you'll probably get your account banned. For fuck's sake, Lewis!'

I hang up and swipe frustrated tears from my eyes. How could he do this? I trusted him. He's the CEO of a hotel. It's so unprofessional. Speaking of which, if Valerie claps eyes on it, I'm going to get a huge rap on the knuckles. Or worse, I could lose my job. She wanted me to be more visible, but not this visible!

Andrea calls, but I ignore her and click back into the TikTok with a shaking hand. It's like a car crash, impossible not to look. There's another 200 likes and thirty more comments. People are still sticking up for me. Plenty of others want to lynch me. I'm afraid if I look outside my window, I'll see a large angry mob shaking their pitchforks and shouting 'Kill the grinch!'

This is not good. What if someone finds out my address and sends it to a Christmas extremist? For my own safety, I can't stay here. It could be dangerous, and I have to think about Crumpet. Who's going to feed him if I get shot?

In a daze, I head towards the hallway and haul my wheelie bag out of the cupboard. Trundling it back to my room, I start packing. Passport—check. Crumpet's favourite squeaky toy, blanket, and lead—check. Sensing something's up, he wanders in and gives an excited woof when he sees me packing his things, thinking we're going on an adventure. *Well, it is, but only to avoid my brains being blown out.*

Andrea calls again.

'Hello,' I mutter, transferring a bundle of underwear from my dresser with one hand.

'Finally! Did you see it?'

'Yes, I saw it. I'm packing.'

'It's not that bad ...' she attempts, but I'm in no mood to be mollified.

'Are you joking? It's worse than bad. I have to leave. There's no other option. If someone hires a hacker, it'll be easy to track me down since he used my first name. I'm not waiting around for a Christmas crazy to knock me off.'

Andrea gives an amused snort. 'I don't think it will get to that, surely! Can't you ask Lewis to take it down?'

'I tried that. No luck. He's buggered off on holiday.'

'Did you report it to TikTok?'

'Yes, and they're looking into it. But I'm not sure how long it will take or if they'll do anything until I'm actively getting death threats. And judging by the tone of some of the comments, that's not far off. If I stay here, I'm going to be a sitting duck.'

'But it's Christmas in two days!' she exclaims.

'No shit, Sherlock.'

'Where are you going to go? I'd say come and hide out at mine until it dies down, but I'm hosting my parents. They're coming up from the Borders tomorrow, and I only have a small flat ...' Andrea trails off.

'Thanks anyway. I don't know. Somewhere. Just not Edinburgh.' I'm too buoyed up on adrenaline to think logically. Cortisol is flowing through my veins, spurring me into flight mode—my preferred method of dealing with confrontation.

'Maybe you're right to get away,' she says. 'TikTok's just the tip of the iceberg.'

My stomach drops like a stone when I realise what she means. With all the shares and repostings, my anti-

Christmas rant could end up being seen all over the internet, in every corner of the globe. This could be life-changing— and not in a good way.

'I'm going to kill him!' I growl, grinding my teeth. Crumpet whines and paws at my leg.

'I have to go. I'm scaring my dog,' I say, putting an abrupt end to our conversation. 'See you on the other side. If you don't hear from me, you'll know I didn't make it.'

Chapter 5

After a whirlwind of packing for a holiday I didn't plan on taking, I run out of steam. After all the exertion, my head is pounding. Maybe I'm being a bit ridiculous. All I have to do is hunker down until Lewis gets my message and deletes the TikTok, then it will all blow over. I'll give it one last check just for peace of mind, and then I won't look at it anymore.

In the kitchen, I stall for time by drinking more water and filling up Crumpet's bowl until I can't put it off any longer. OK, let's see it.

The TikTok has reached 1.5 million views, with 100,000 likes and 3,000 comments.

With mounting dread, I force myself to read them. It's the usual until I see something that makes my stomach start churning like a cake mixer. Someone thinks they know me, and there's a whole comment thread about it and then a confirmation:

It's Holly Driver. I used to work with her. Roflmao.

Nauseous from the stress and last night's binge drinking, I throw up the meagre contents of my stomach into the sink.

Leaning against the counter, I wipe my sweaty face with a tea towel and groan. Shit, I've been outed. This is not good.

There are no messages from Lewis or TikTok admin. Everyone's on holiday now—kicking back, relaxing with their partners, families, and kids while wrapping presents, eating mince pies, drinking mulled wine, and singing ra pa pum pum. Too bad about me dealing with a social media shit show. Well. Fuck. Them.

'Come on, Crumpet, we're leaving—now!'

Wheelie and mini schnauzer in tow, and battling my chronic hangover, I set off determinedly towards Waverley station. I'm glad I had the foresight to wear my thickest coat and combat boots. The air is bitterly cold, and the sky is gunmetal grey, threatening snow. It's nearing noon, and I haven't booked a train ticket. But surely, the station won't be that busy?

Wrong. At Waverley, there's a horde of people jostling through the entranceway. I haven't thought this through at all. 'Stay close to me, mate.' Luckily, Crumpet's obedient when he's clipped on, and he hates crowds as much as me. I grip his lead tightly and plunge in towards the main concourse. With all the chattering and suitcase wheels juddering, my headache is roaring. Focus. Get a ticket. Get on a train. Get out of Edinburgh. But where to?

I gaze at the departure board with its confusing mass of

place names. Then one jumps out: Inverness. There's a train leaving in fifteen minutes. I've been there. It was before I had Crumpet, but the guest house I stayed in didn't mind dogs because I distinctly remember a labradoodle in the dining room and everyone wanting to pet it. If that one's booked, I'm sure there'll be others. Relief flows through me. I have a plan. Head north. Stay at a random guest house that takes dogs. I'll book it on the train. Simple.

Unlocking my phone, I click on the Trainline app. There's one ticket left. It's eye-wateringly expensive, but I pay for it. It's all coming together. I'm even starting to look forward to the adventure. We can go for walks, visit Culloden, maybe take a boat trip out on Loch Ness. I'm not due back at work until after New Year's, so I can even stay up there for Hogmanay. By the time I get back, after all the family and Christmas drama that is bound to happen between now and then, the TikTok will be old news.

Our journey doesn't get off to the best start when I board the wrong end of the carriage and have to push through people crowding the aisles with their bags of presents. Everyone is exclaiming over Crumpet, and there are hands reaching out to pet him, interfering with his lead. So trying to juggle my wheelie and keep him moving forward is an effort.

When I eventually get to where I'm supposed to be, I'm

faced with two girls in their twenties—one of them sitting by the window and the other in my aisle seat.

'Hi, I'm meant to be in there,' I say to her, showing the confirmation on my phone.

The girl looks up at me. 'Would you mind possibly swapping seats so my friend and I can sit here?' She smiles engagingly, as if it shouldn't be any trouble on my part to do what she wants.

'Where is it?' I ask, not returning the smile.

'Over there,' she says, pointing to a four-seater table with a guy cradling a plastic bag of Tennent's Lager cans, one of which he's steadily slurping from; and the train hasn't even left yet.

'No thanks,' I reply. 'I'm not sitting across from him for the next three hours.' The smell of his lager belches will make me hurl.

'I think he's getting off at Perth,' she hedges, but I'm in no mood to be trifled with.

'No, sorry.' I'm polite, but firm.

'Oh, come on,' her friend says. 'It's Christmas!' Like that's supposed to change anything. All it does is piss me off.

'That seat just cost me £150, and I'm not paying that much to sit next to a lager-swilling lout. So please move. Or I can fetch the conductor, and he'll sort it out.'

There's much sighing and heaving of crop top bosoms and flouncing of hair, but both of them vacate and push off down the carriage, looking for alternative seats. 'Bitch' floats back to me, but I don't really give a rat's ass. I've got more pressing problems, like 1.5 million people who've seen me drunkenly ranting in a shower cap. Besides, now I've got two seats to myself. Bonus.

Stowing my bag on the rack above, I settle in next to the window with Crumpet under my feet. I glance out and catch a flash of someone with golden-brown hair wearing a red jumper. My nerves ping. Was that just ...? I really hope not. I peer cautiously over the seats in front to see if anyone boards the carriage. That's all I need, that guy Bailey to be on the same train as me. But no one comes in, and I relax again. It must've just been someone who looks like him, and there are Christmas jumpers galore around at the moment.

The two girls are back, unable to find two more seats together on the full train. They sit across from the lager-swilling dude, whispering together and looking at their phones, then over at me. I'm probably being paranoid, but there's a good chance they've seen the TikTok if it's gone supernova. My anxiety levels kick up a notch just thinking about it. Don't look at it. Just forget about it. I need to concentrate on booking a guest house in Inverness. Otherwise, we're going to be sleeping under a bridge. There are slim pickings. One by the river has a double room, but they don't mention if pets are OK. I ring to check and have a brief conversation with the receptionist. 'No, sorry, love. Dogs mean extra work for the staff.'

'But he's very clean. He's cleaner than me!'

'I'm sure he is, but that's our policy.'

'Well, you should put that on your site,' I mutter. 'It's not a good user experience.'

After searching the online nooks and crannies of Inverness, the best I can come up with is a single room in a one-star guest house on the outskirts of town. Threadbare brown carpet. Thin flowered curtains. Flat beige pillows and a one-bar heater. But I can have Crumpet in with me, and it's a free breakfast.

'What's that entail?' I ask the barely comprehensible man who answers the phone.

'Beans, toast, an' egg, if yer lucky. Might be able tae do yer a bit o' bacon since it's Christmas an' all.'

So much for a fun stay in Inverness.

I don't really have a choice. 'Fine. I'll take it for four nights.'

The train trundles northward through white fields, and big fluffy flakes drift from the sky. I do like snow, I have to admit, so it's a treat to see a big dumping. I hold Crumpet up to the window. 'Look, buddy, snow!'

Crumpet licks the glass, and I give him some water (not too much, don't want him peeing everywhere) and take a swallow myself. This hangover is never-ending. I'm craving a good night's sleep and a shower. The thought of the tiny hovel in Inverness that awaits isn't pleasant, but it's better than nothing.

Overcome with exhaustion, the swaying motion of the train lulls me, and I nod off with my head propped against the window. When I wake up sometime later, the train isn't moving, and we're stopped at a station—Kingussie, the sign says. Snow is falling faster now, and it's almost dark outside, since it's nearing 3 p.m. I yawn and stretch my stiff neck.

'Ugh, another hour to go,' I tell Crumpet, who's curled on the seat next to me. He thumps his tail and doesn't look too concerned. Maybe I can take him for a quick walk in the fresh air, but it looks freezing out there, and it's warm in here.

I rise to stretch my legs, then notice there isn't actually anyone in the carriage. It's completely empty, and there's no luggage in the racks apart from my suitcase. What the?

A conductor comes in, whistling, and stops when he sees me. 'Oh, didn't you hear the announcement? Everyone off the train.'

'I was asleep. What's going on?'

'A line issue because of the snow. There's a rail replacement bus to Inverness. You should hurry, though, if you want to catch it. Cute dog.' He carries on down the carriage.

Oh god, just what I need—an hour on a bus. Groggily, I get my belongings together, shrug on my coat, and heft down my wheelie. 'Why didn't you wake me, Crumpet?' I grumble to him, and he whines. It wasn't his fault. He was asleep too.

Outside the station, there's a bus rumbling in neutral with its exhaust belching steam into the crisp air. The bus door is closed. I rap smartly; and it opens, blowing a puff of warm air in my face, to reveal a bearded man in a tartan vest.

'Can I come on?'

'Sorry, love, I'm full. You'll have to catch a taxi like the others.' He nods at the shivering line of people outside the station. A taxi? Seriously? That's going to cost a fortune.

'Is there another bus coming?'

He shrugs.

'Surely, there's one seat available. My dog can sit on my lap.'

He shakes his head. 'Sorry, safety regulations.' He closes the door in my face, puts the bus into gear, and it starts moving slowly off. The two annoying girls from the train are sitting at the back, staring at me out the window. One of them grins maliciously and gives me the finger. Charming.

There's no way I'm waiting in the snow for a taxi. Besides, Crumpet is shivering. I tuck him inside my coat and wander back to the waiting room, which is warm at least. OK, plan B. I'll find a guest house in Kingussie and stay the night here. But the accommodation gods aren't playing ball. There's zilch on the booking sites and nothing on Airbnb either. Kingussie is a blip on the map, and it's two days before Christmas, so I'm not sure why I think there would be. But I'm not in my right mind. It's now pitch-black outside. Train passengers start piling back into the station—brushing white flakes off their coats, stamping ice off boots, and grumbling about the state of the Scottish rail system.

'Are there no taxis?' I ask a woman who passes by.

'Seems not. There's only one company, and no one is answering. It just keeps ringing.'

'Maybe they'll send another bus?'

She shakes her head. 'It's a disgrace, AND it's nearly Christmas. I've got a defrosting ham that needs to go in the fridge. It'll be ruined!' she exclaims.

'You could always put it out in the snow,' I suggest helpfully.

She just looks at me like I'm mad and tramps off.

Well, I guess we're all spending the night in the train

station. At this point, the hovel in Inverness with its flat beige pillows is starting to look appealing. My phone notifies me I've got an email from TikTok admin. Finally! It's brief and to the point, saying they're trying to contact the owner of the account. They can't ban it in the meantime as, from the looks of the content, I was actively participating and knew what I was doing. However, if it has been posted without my consent, that is a different matter. So I have to wait for them to talk to Lewis.

Aargh.

I bury my face in my hands. Nothing's going right! I breathe through my nose in shallow bursts, feeling a panic attack coming on. I'm stuck in the middle of nowhere with a bunch of disgruntled strangers, no food, and half a bottle of water. I've fucked up this trip. But I fucked up in the first place because I trusted Lewis. I thought he was interested in getting to know me as a person, but he just wanted to use me for entertainment. I let my guard down, and he threw me to the wolves.

I'm busy lamenting my fate when a pair of Nike runners and jean-clad legs appear in front of me. 'I'm not interested,' I mumble, thinking it's some do-gooder who wants to chat.

The jeans legs and runners don't move.

I glance up through splayed fingers and stare directly into the black beady eyes of a gingerbread man.

Chapter 6

'Hi ... Holly, isn't it? Well, this is weird.'

Oh crappity crap. It *was* Bailey. He's standing right in front of me with a quizzical look on his face. He's wearing a red jumper with a waving gingerbread man, a black coat, and a red-and-white knitted scarf tied loosely around his neck. There's a light dusting of snow on his golden-brown hair. I stare at him in shock, trying to form a sentence, but my brain is not prepared for this further horror.

'I didn't recognise you without the elf ears,' I finally say sarcastically.

But he grins good-naturedly. 'I only wear them for special occasions.'

Since I've been squeezing him in annoyance, Crumpet wriggles out of my coat and jumps onto the floor.

'Oh wow. Who's this?' Bailey crouches down to pet him, and Crumpet disloyally licks his hand. I pull him back to me.

'Crumpet.'

'Hey, Crumpet. Hey, girl.'

'It's a *he*,' I correct smartly.

'Oh, sorry.' Bailey stands up and puts his hands in his coat pockets. 'So where are you off to? Home for Christmas?'

I nod once. He peers at me inquisitively, hoping to get more information, and I sigh. He's so annoying. OK, we're doing this. Conversing.

'Yes, Inverness. My, er ... grandmother's.' It's kind of true. My biological grandmother is from Inverness. She may still be alive, but she's more than likely dead. 'Well, I was until the train came to an abrupt halt. What about you?'

'Ballindalloch. Dad's picking me up. I was waiting outside, but he just rang to say he had to stop and put on snow chains, so he's going to be late. Isn't it funny that we were on the same train?'

'Hilarious,' I say.

'How come you didn't get on the rail replacement bus?' Bailey glances at the chair next to me like he wants to sit down, but I plonk my handbag on it so he doesn't get any ideas.

'It's a long story. I don't want to bore you.'

'I'm not easily bored.'

Hmm, maybe I'll tell him the shortened version. 'I got home late from the party last night, and I fell asleep on the train. When I woke up, everyone had gone from my carriage, and the bus was full. So now I'm deciding what to do next.'

Bailey frowns. 'Strange. I never saw you again after we first met, and I was at the party until at least eleven.'

I hesitate. He obviously hasn't seen the TikTok, or he would've mentioned it. Bailey doesn't seem like the type of guy to have a filter.

'I was around,' I say vaguely. Best to change the subject. 'How do you know Lewis anyway?'

He shrugs. 'I'm head chef at the hotel.' Great. Looks like we're both connected with Lewis professionally. I'll need to tread carefully. If he's friends with him, he'll probably take Lewis's side.

His phone vibrates, and he checks it. 'Dad's nearly here,' he says, and I don't reply. Great for him.

He gazes at me, and I look away, feeling scrutinised again. He has a habit of doing that, like he's trying to get under my skin. I don't like it.

'I feel bad leaving you here with no way to get to Inverness,' he says.

'It's not your problem,' I reply. 'I'm sure another bus or some taxis will turn up.' I'm not hopeful on either of those things occurring, but I don't need his pity.

'Are you sure?' Bailey doesn't seem convinced. 'You could come and stay the night with us? I can run you into Inverness tomorrow. It's only an hour from Ballindalloch.'

I start protesting, but he's made up his mind.

'No, I think it's better if you do ... Lewis will never let me hear the end of it if I leave his project manager stranded in Kingussie.'

Huh, somehow, I don't think Lewis will give a shit.

'Besides, it's freezing, and it's Christmas.' Why do people keep saying that? Is Christmas the only time you're meant to be kind and helpful? You can be an arsehole any other time of year, but if it's Christmas, you should buck up your ideas?

'Your dog looks like he could do with some food and water too.'

I look at Crumpet, who stares back at me with woeful doggy eyes, and my resolve cracks. Damn, he's got me there.

'OK ... for Crumpet,' I finally agree. Actually, I'm relieved he's offered and is being insistent about it. My thumping headache has returned, my eyes feel sore and scratchy, and I could murder a cup of tea.

We only have to wait a few minutes outside the station when a black Range Rover with a snowy roof pulls up next to us, its windscreen wipers going full bore to stave off the ice. A man with a short grey beard, a tweed flat cap, and a Barbour jacket gets out, leaving the car running, and comes over to us.

'Hey, Dad.' Bailey and his father hug. The man looks at

me and smiles, his grey eyes crinkling. 'Who's this, Bails? You made a friend?' he asks.

'This is Holly. She's with me,' Bailey replies. I wait for him to clarify that statement to his father, but he doesn't. Before I can say anything, I'm pulled into a quick rough hug by the man, and I realise with a shock, *He thinks I'm his girlfriend!*

'We'd better get going, Bails. I have a feeling they might close the road if this gets any worse. I'll pop the boot for your bags. Can you check the snow chains on the back wheels? I did them in a hurry.'

Bailey nods and beckons me to the rear of the Range Rover so we can load our bags. Despite the arctic temperature, my face is flaming hot. Why didn't he explain to his father? Bailey picks up my wheelie bag and pretends to stagger under its weight. 'What have you got in here? Bricks?' he jokes.

I clutch my handbag tightly to my chest. 'Just a few books!'

'Ah.' He inserts my bag beside some paint tins and a pile of rope, then places his own khaki canvas knapsack on top. I note it has some Christmas-themed badges sewn on: a candy cane, a Santa sock, an elf, and a snowman. Wow, this guy really is a festive freak.

'Why the *hell* did you let your dad think we were

together?' I splutter under my breath as Bailey reaches up a hand to pull down the boot door. He closes the boot and glances at me.

'Just go with it. There's a good reason. You'll see why when we arrive.'

'I cannot fathom any reason why you would say that. Unless you're fully psycho, like Norman Bates in a gingerbread man jumper.'

He seems unfazed at my jibe, but there's something about the intense way he's looking at me that makes me pause before berating him further. 'You should get in the car. Your eyelashes are starting to collect snow,' he says quietly.

'Fine,' I mutter. 'But you've got some explaining to do.'

Wiping snowflakes from my eyes, I yank open the rear door, and Crumpet jumps up onto the back seat. His paws leave a trail of ice and wet prints on the black upholstery. Bailey's dad half turns and smiles at him. 'Well, hello there. We used to have a mini schnauzer,' he says to me conversationally. 'Rupert, his name was. He died only recently. Bailey loved him. Then again, he loves all animals. Let's see, when he was little, he had a turtle, a rabbit, a hamster, a cat. Then later on, Rupert, of course.' He ticks them off on his fingers.

I nod, a bit amused. Wow, I'm getting the full rundown

on Bailey's childhood menagerie before he's even got in the car. I can see where Bailey gets his no-filter personality from.

'What's your dog's name?'

'Crumpet,' I reply.

'Brilliant. Well, you're both very welcome.'

How long does he think I'm staying?

I remember my manners. 'Thanks for having us, Mr ...' I begin, then realise I don't even know Bailey's last name.

'Just call me Allan, Holly,' he says pleasantly. 'After all, we're practically family now.'

Bailey jumps in the front seat amidst a flurry of snow.

'Oof, let's go. It's getting worse,' he says. His dad puts the Range Rover in gear, and we crunch off slowly through the snow, leaving behind the lit-up station with its collection of stranded travellers. A small part of me is grateful for bumping into Bailey and that I'm going to have somewhere to sleep other than the station floor. The other much larger part of me is fuming that he let his dad believe we're a couple.

'All right back there?' Bailey twists his head and gives me a dimpled grin. But I scowl at him, and he faces the front again hurriedly.

'So how long have you two been an item?' his dad asks.

'Not long,' says Bailey casually. 'It's been a bit of a

whirlwind romance.' I clench my fists tightly, quietly seething, but manage to hold my tongue. There'd better be a bloody good reason for this!

'It must've been,' says his dad, 'since you haven't mentioned her to us at all. No offence, Holly.'

'None taken,' I say gruffly, curious to hear what Bailey will say to that.

But he just replies airily, 'We were waiting until the right time. Christmas seemed like the perfect occasion.'

What the hell is he playing at? I check his profile, and there's a small smile playing on his lips, which makes me uneasy. I'm not sure what I'm getting myself into by agreeing to come home with him.

'Are the others there yet?' he asks his father.

Others?

'Simon, Kate, and company arrived late last night. And Mirabelle's flight was delayed coming in from Paris, so she'll be here tomorrow morning. And Sarah came up by train yesterday with the girls.'

'Who are Simon and Kate? And Mirabelle and Sarah?' I venture, trying to get a handle on who's going to be at the house.

Allan shakes his head and tsks at Bailey. 'You haven't told her about your siblings?'

'Er, no,' he says. 'I didn't get around to that.'

Allan glances at me through the rear-vision mirror. 'Simon is Bailey's elder brother, and Kate is his wife. They have three boys: Noah, Silas, and Tyrone. And Sarah is his elder sister. She and her partner, Mirabelle, have two girls, Susie and Sasha. Mirabelle works in Paris, but they have a house in London.'

I start feeling a bit stressed trying to keep track of all the names.

'But that's just the tip of the iceberg ...' Allan adds with a laugh.

My heart rate increases. 'W-what do you mean?'

'Dad!' says Bailey sharply. 'We don't want to scare her off.'

Too late. I'm scared.

I stare at the door handle longingly, wondering if I can jump out now and make a run for it.

Chapter 7

After an hour of driving through rural countryside, with me getting more and more anxious about where we're going, we pull through an open gate and into a driveway lined with spruce trees coated in snow.

I lean forward as a two-storey stone house with dormer windows and chimneys comes into view through the windscreen wipers. At first, I think it's a cottage. But as we get nearer, it becomes apparent it's much larger. I count ten windows on the front alone. Thick snow covers the roof like white frosting on a cake.

But that's not what makes me gape in disbelief. Someone has gone to town with the Christmas lights. They're flashing all over the front of the house in alternating strobes of blue, red, yellow, and green. One side of the front lawn has a ten-foot-tall fake snowman with a pipe. The other has a reindeer ensemble pulling a sleigh. And as we drive past, I spot an inflatable Santa attached to the side of the house—in climb mode.

'Oh. My. God,' I say aloud without thinking.

Allan bursts out laughing. 'Aye, we get into Christmas in

a big way in our family. It's the one time of year when you can go a bit crazy. Fun, isn't it?'

I can think of other words for it.

As we crunch to a stop, the front door opens, and my eyes widen at the steady stream of people that come piling out heading towards the car.

Suddenly, Bailey and I are standing outside in the snow, and I'm being hugged and asked questions simultaneously. I'm introduced to so many people I can't remember all of their names. I just nod in a daze. Little kids are running around everywhere, kicking up flurries, laughing, and chattering. Some are making snow angels. Crumpet scampers off with a woof and joins them. Traitor. There are multiple piercing cries of 'Uncle Bailey, look at me! Uncle Bailey!'

I wince as my eardrums threaten to burst.

'Yikes, they've been inside all afternoon. Simon just opened a bag of mini chocolate Santas, so they're on a sugar high,' comments a young woman around my age who's just joined the throng. She has long blonde hair and is wearing a pink knitted beanie. She smiles at me kindly and doesn't try to hug me, for which I'm grateful.

'Hi, I'm Sarah, Bailey's sister. This must be a bit overwhelming for you. Why don't we leave them to it and go inside where it's warm and have a cup of tea?'

I nod, feeling relieved, and let her shepherd me into the house, leaving the noise and chaos behind us.

We walk down a long corridor with uneven wood flooring. The walls are covered in photos. The house smells of wax polish mixed with undercurrents of spice and pine.

'This used to be an old schoolhouse,' Sarah tells me. 'Our parents bought and renovated it around thirty years ago, just before Bailey was born. They needed somewhere cheap to house and raise their brood.'

'It's massive,' I say, gazing up at the high peaked ceiling.

'It seems that way, but there's a special nook where you can escape to read a book or think your own thoughts. I'll show you later,' says Sarah.

I open my mouth to tell her I'm only here for the night but then close it again. I'm not sure I should be saying anything. Bailey obviously has some kind of master plan in play. I'll wait and see what it is.

'This is the kitchen. And Mum.'

A tall woman in a forest-green jumper and skinny jeans turns from the counter, where she's been chopping something. She has thick shoulder-length golden-brown hair threaded with grey. She's slim, but there's something strong and capable about her—like she wouldn't stand for any nonsense, but if you skinned your knee, she'd instantly be sympathetic and ready with the plasters.

She smiles at me, and her round cheeks dimple like Bailey's. She has his snub nose as well. 'Hello, you're a new face.'

'She's with Bailey,' Sarah explains, and I stiffen when I see his mother instantly brighten. Oh no.

'Ah ... *I see*!' She comes over, wiping her hands on a tea towel, and I feel like the biggest fraud ever. I'm going to tear a strip off him when I see him next.

'Well, he kept that quiet. But welcome, welcome. I'm Jennifer.'

'Holly,' I supply.

She looks like she's about to have kittens. 'Holly! You even have a Christmassy name—that is so perfect for him.'

'Mum, Holly needs a cup of tea,' Sarah says gently. 'She's just met everyone, and you know how exhausting that can be.' I'm starting to like this girl. She seems to know exactly the right thing to say.

'Of course. Take a seat, Holly, and I'll put the kettle on. Sarah, do you want one?'

'Yes please. Sit here with me,' she says, pulling out a couple of chairs at the well-scrubbed kitchen table, and I flop into one in relief.

I'm halfway through a strong cup of tea and feeling more human when Bailey appears with our bags, one in each hand, and dumps them in the kitchen. He unwinds his scarf, and a small waterfall of white sludge slides off and starts melting on the slate tiles.

'Whoops!' he says, stepping over it. 'Hi, Mum. Sorry about the puddle. I was making snow angels with the kids.'

He goes to give her a hug, which she returns, then whacks him lightly around the shoulders. I stare, fascinated.

'Bailey,' she chides.

'What? I'll clean it up.' He reaches for the tea towel.

'No, not that! Poor Holly is overwhelmed. You could've at least warned her.'

Bailey chuckles, and his dimples appear briefly. Grrr, I wish he wasn't so wholesome. He would be easier to hate if he didn't look like a cheeky 12-year-old. 'Och, no, she's not.'

I clear my throat. 'Yes, I am actually,' I tell him. 'I may need a flow chart to get my head around your family. How many siblings do you actually have?'

Everyone laughs. But I'm deadly serious. That was a fuckload of people in the driveway.

'I've got two brothers and two sisters, and then there's their partners and offspring, so I think we're at eighteen for this Christmas.'

Jennifer and Sarah nod to confirm it. My mouth drops open, contemplating Jennifer's trim physique. 'You've had *five* kids? But you look so young and thin.'

It sounds a bit rude, but she smiles and does a little curtsy.

'Thank you. Bailey put an end to the baby production line. There was no way I was going to go through that again. Ten pounds, what a heffalump!'

She ruffles his hair affectionately, and I wash down my own heffalump of envy that's formed in my throat with the rest of my tea. I stand up abruptly.

'I should ring my grandmother and let her know I'm not coming 'til tomorrow.'

'But aren't you staying for Christmas?' Jennifer asks, sounding surprised.

'No, only for tonight. She has her own family celebrations to attend,' says Sarah smoothly.

She seems to have been well briefed by Bailey on my movements. I'm not sure when that happened. The part between my leaving the car and making it into the house is a blur of noise and confusion.

'Ah, well, that's a shame,' says Jennifer, her eyes twinkling. 'But at least we have you for one night.'

I'm surprised that she genuinely seems to mean it. People usually aren't so enthusiastic about having me join their gatherings. It makes me suspicious.

'If you want to freshen up before dinner, the bathroom is right next door to Bailey's room ...' Jennifer continues. 'Or feel free to take a nap. I put an extra quilt on his bed, so you should both be quite snuggly in there.'

The blood drains from my face as her meaning sinks in. Fuckity fuck. She's assumed we're sleeping together! I give Bailey an icy glare, and he must see I'm about to lose my rag because he says quickly, 'I'll go up with Holly, then come back and help you with dinner, Mum.'

I note then that there are a number of cast-iron saucepans waiting on the counter and an enormous Aga stove. Feeding this family must take a hell of a lot of organisation, but I guess they're used to it. And Bailey said he's head chef at the hotel, so he must have the necessary skills.

'Speaking of food, I don't suppose you have a spare bone for Crumpet ...?' I say, feeling bad for asking.

'Who's Crumpet?' enquires Jennifer.

'Holly's mini schnauzer,' answers Sarah. 'Don't worry, I'll look after him. We have some dog food in the pantry.'

So there's nothing left for me to do but grab the handle of my bag and stalk into the hallway with Bailey following close behind. When we're out of earshot, I round on him.

'This is going too far. First, I'm your girlfriend, and now I'm sleeping in your bed? There's no way *that's* happening,' I say through gritted teeth.

Bailey shoots a swift look at the kitchen door and grabs

my bag.

'Not here, I'll explain in the room.' He practically runs up the stairs, leaving me no choice but to follow.

'This better be bloody good,' I mutter.

At the top of the stairs, there's a beige carpeted landing with still more family photos. I glimpse Bailey heading into one of the end rooms, so I trail after him, determined to get some answers.

Bailey's room is cosy with a queen-sized bed made up with a white duvet and a yellow quilt. Model airplanes hang from the ceiling. A row of teddy bears sits on a shelf. On one whitewashed wall, there's a large corkboard with photos tacked to it. On the other, a life-sized poster of Justin Timberlake. The entire room is a nod to his past, but I'm not in the mood to be sentimental. I close the door behind me and lean against it with folded arms. This is as far as I'm going until I get some answers.

'Right, tell me now.'

Bailey dumps my bag on one side of the bed and stows his own on an easy chair with a crocheted blanket draped over it.

'It's nothing to get riled up about,' he says. 'If we weren't together, you'd get put with the kids in the lounge. That's all.'

'So? It's only for one night.'

'You don't understand,' Bailey says patiently. 'It's not a peaceful experience where everyone goes quietly off to sleep. They'll ask you for bedtime stories and to take them to the bathroom at 3 a.m., and at 4 a.m. You'll get fingers in your eyeballs, and someone will jump on you and land on your bladder. Then when you finally doze off, they're awake at 5 a.m. and chasing each other round the room. They're little monsters. I'm doing you a favour.'

'But can't I bunk in with Sarah? Her partner isn't arriving until tomorrow ...'

'They're in the box room, and there's only a double bed. And I'm sure you've already figured out that Sarah is a lesbian. So it's not appropriate.'

'So it's more appropriate to be in here with you when we're actually *not* together?' I scoff.

He rubs his hand over his face, as if I'm tiring him out. 'Trust me, yes, even if you don't want to be. As you say, it's just for one night. You'll be gone tomorrow.'

'Sounds like you can't wait,' I grumble.

Bailey rolls his eyes heavenwards. 'I can't win with you.'

'You could sleep on the floor?' I suggest, not really liking the idea of sharing a bed with him. What if he snores or, even worse, sleeps nude? Ugh, my skin crawls just thinking about it.

'No way, it's wooden floorboards. I'm not that much of

a gentleman. If it makes you feel better, we can put a barrier down the middle.' He gestures to the mound of colourful display cushions adorning the top of the bed.

'Fine.' My eyelids are starting to feel like lead weights, and I can't be bothered arguing. After the day I've had, the bed is starting to look appealing even if it is only 4.30 p.m. I stifle a yawn. 'I might have a nap.'

'Sure, I'll leave you to it. I need to help with dinner anyway.' We gingerly swap places, Bailey heading towards the door and me to the bed.

'Just one question.'

'Yes?' He turns, and since I'm now sitting on the bed, the gingerbread man on his jumper is level with my head. I ignore its stupid beady eyes.

'What happens after I leave tomorrow? When your family never sees me again, I mean. Won't they think it's weird?'

'Oh.' Bailey frowns, as if he's thinking. 'I'll just tell them we broke up in the New Year. They won't be offended. They'll probably forget all about you.'

'But ... but your mum seemed pleased you had a girlfriend, like *really* pleased. What's with that?' *And they seemed to quite like me, which was even odder.*

He shrugs. 'I guess I haven't been out with anyone for a while.' I wait for him to elaborate, but he doesn't. His ears have gone a faint shade of pink, though.

Fair enough, I'm not going to probe into his personal life. It's not like we're friends or anything. I'm just a random girl he met last night who's let his family think he's dating so I can get a decent night's sleep. What a guy. I'm not entirely convinced Bailey's intentions are pure, but all I can do is just go with it at this point and be on my guard.

'So I'll come and get you in an hour. Dinner's not 'til seven, but you can help me make my special Christmas trifle if you like.'

I yawn again. 'What's so special about it?'

Bailey taps the side of his snub nose. 'It has a secret ingredient.'

Rum or whisky probably. The thought of ingesting anything involving alcohol after last night makes me balk. I kick off my shoes and reach for the quilt. 'I don't like trifle,' I say resolutely.

His mouth quirks. 'Trust me, you'll like this one.'

Hmmm, he seems to say that a lot. But trusting him is **not** something I intend on doing.

Chapter 8

I lie on the bed, staring up at the model airplane swinging directly above my head. Now I'm alone, I'm not sleepy. My nerves are on edge being in a strange room in a strange house with strange people, and I'm feeling bad at leaving Crumpet with said strangers. He's a pretty well-adjusted dog, but meeting this many people at once could be beyond his socialisation skills.

Far below, I hear the muffled slam of a door and a muted rumble of voices, like a noisy TV show turned to low volume. The horde must be back inside. My eyes flick to a corkboard with photos tacked to it—a montage of Bailey's life, I assume. I'm not going to have a nosey at that. Well ... maybe just a quick glance so I know who I'm dealing with.

At first glance, the photos seem to be based around a particularly epic camping trip. Someone got snap-happy and decided to document it in great detail. I start at the top and work my way down. The first one shows the six campers, three guys and three girls in their mid-twenties, standing with arms linked in front of a pile of camping gear in a living room. Then there are several photos of hiking poses and Highland scenery. It must be summer since they're all in T-shirts and shorts. Bailey is easy to spot. He's in practically every photo. His hair is longer, and he looks slightly younger, but it's definitely him. I'd recognise that grin anywhere.

As the photos continue, Bailey seems to be the sole focus. In one, he's on his own in the kitchen at the table, slurping Pot Noodles. In another, he's lying on a couch with his feet up. There's another of him standing legs astride, looking out over a valley. Hmm, someone seemed to like taking photos of him. I reach the bottom, and the last one is a selfie of him and a pretty brown-haired girl with rosy cheeks and plaits. They're both beaming at the camera. Strangely, I feel a small twist in my gut as I realise she's the one who's been taking the photos. An ex-girlfriend? Did they get together on the camping trip? They're obviously not together anymore. Otherwise, she'd be the one sleeping in his bed, not me. Backing away from the corkboard, I stretch out on the bed again. Maybe he had his heart broken by her. That's why he hasn't been out with anyone for a while—

My musings about Bailey's love life are interrupted by my phone vibrating in my jeans pocket.

'Hello?'

'Is this Holly Driver? You made a booking today for a four-night stay at the Cumberfeldy Inn. I'm ringing tae see if yer actually coming.' The man I spoke to earlier sounds disgruntled, but it could be just his personality.

'Oh. Uh, thanks. I had train trouble, so I'm staying with a … friend tonight. Sorry, I should've called earlier.'

He sniffs. 'So you still want the room then? Otherwise, I'll have tae cancel it.'

'No, I still want it. I'm coming tomorrow.' However, after this comfy room, the thought of the Inverness guest house makes me shrink a little. It doesn't seem like much fun. But everything else is booked up. 'I'll still pay for tonight, of course.'

'Aye, good to hear. And t' breakfast too.'

'But I thought it was free?'

'I had to go t' shops, specially for t' can o' beans and t' bacon. So I've added it to t' room cost. Plus a service charge for ma trouble,' he says.

Wonderful, now I'm paying for a room and food at a shitty guest house, and I'm not actually even there!

After talking to the man, my headache returns, so I close my eyes to rest them. I must fall asleep as I'm woken by a snuffling noise. Crumpet has nosed the door open and jumped onto the bed. I put up a hand to stroke his silky ears.

'Hey, buddy. Have they been looking after you?'

My hand touches his collar, and I discover someone has

tied a green tinsel bow on it. That's annoying. I pull it off and find a folded note tucked underneath with a message:

Come down to the kitchen, your apron awaits. B

'Cute, very cute. He's sending you to do his dirty work for him, I see.' Crumpet is exhausted from all the people making a fuss of him, so I leave him curled up on the quilt to have a snooze.

On my way back to the kitchen, I pass a lounge off the downstairs hallway and peer in. Children are involved in various activities: A boy is huddled over an iPad. A few more are playing board games. A slightly older girl is sitting on a window seat, reading a book. The feral children I've been saved from, I assume. They seem reasonably well behaved to me.

Next to the kitchen, another open door reveals a dining room with an oval table with a snow-white linen cloth and silver candlesticks. To my mind, it doesn't look big enough to fit eighteen people. Even twelve is too much. I hate crowds. Before entering the kitchen, which is emitting a steady hum of chatter, I take a deep breath. *It's a free bed and a free meal.*

I push open the kitchen door; and a thrum of warmth, light, and energy envelops me. To my relief, it's only Bailey's brother Kirk and sister Hazel and Sarah's girls, Sasha and Susie, whom I did meet previously, but I forgot who was who since they're identical twins. Bailey's sister-in-law, Kate, waves at me from a corner chair over by the window, where she's breastfeeding a child. There's no sign of Jennifer, Allan or Sarah.

'Um, hi?' I venture.

There's a general commotion of welcome. Hazel and Kirk have been talking and drinking cups of tea in chairs in front of the Aga while the girls are colouring in books at their feet on the mat. Cast-iron saucepans simmer on the cook top, and a pie with golden brown pastry and bubbling edges is giving off a delicious aroma from the oven.

Ignoring my rumbling tummy, I head over to Bailey, who has his hands in a bowl at the kitchen table.

As I approach, he smiles. 'Hey, you're awake. Did you get my note?'

'Yes, I did.' I blink at his hands, which are covered in red stuff. 'Did you murder someone?'

He laughs. 'Not yet. I'm just washing these berries. They've collapsed a bit.'

I slip a nearby black apron over my head, and he looks approving. I glance down and sigh. There's a giant pink-and-white candy cane appliquéd on the front. Of course he would like it.

A few of the kids from the other room come running in to ask when dinner's ready and get shooed out again with promises of 'soon'. I feel something grabbing my leg and look down to see a miniature version of Bailey staring back up at me with wide brown eyes.

'Mamma?' he asks.

'No, I'm not your mamma,' I say, giving my leg a shake.

'Mamma!' he says more insistently. I jerk my leg harder, trying to remove him, but he won't budge. He has an iron grip.

'Er ... who's this kid's mamma?' I ask in general to the room, which causes the twins to giggle. Hazel gently pries his fingers from my jeans.

'Sorry, he's mine. He tends to get clingy at this time of night. Come on, Charlie, let's go and see what Amy's doing, shall we?' She scoops him up, and they exit the room. Charlie stares at me over his mum's shoulder with his thumb in his mouth.

'All right?' asks Bailey, who's been watching the scene.

'Fine,' I say neutrally. 'What do you want me to do?'

'Whip the cream?'

'I think I can manage that.'

When I've finished whipping the cream, Bailey hands me a Tesco Strawberry and Cream Swiss Roll, saying, 'Something I prepared earlier. I was too busy to make one.'

He goes over to a cupboard and brings down a fancy cut glass bowl.

'Who's cooking Christmas dinner at the hotel if you're here?' I ask.

'We've got a substitute chef who steps in when I'm on holiday. Can you cut the sponge into slices?'

I do as I'm told, but out of the corner of my eye, I happen to see Kate finish feeding and bounce her kid on her knee. She doesn't bother covering herself. I feel a bit shocked. Doesn't she care that her boob is hanging out for all and sundry to see? I sneak a glance at Bailey, who's arranging the sponge slices around the side of the bowl.

I clear my throat nervously, and he looks up.

'You OK?'

'Three o'clock. Kate. Boob,' I mutter under my breath.

He glances over and shrugs. 'No big deal. We don't care about that stuff. We've been brought up to be comfortable with nudity, probably because Mum and Dad are naturists.'

I gape at him. 'They're *what*?'

Bailey nods. 'Aye, big time. In fact, they're out there now communing with nature. Simon and Sarah are with them too. They like to dabble when they visit.'

I can't get my head around this.

People are *naked* in the *snow*! 'But it's flipping freezing out there! Are they mad?'

Bailey spoons berries into the bowl to make the bottom layer of the trifle. 'Nah, they find it bracing. It's like wild swimming, gets the blood pumping. And they're wearing wellingtons and hats.' He jerks his chin towards the back door. 'They should be back any minute to warm up. You can ask them about it.'

I stare at the door, my mind boggling. What kind of family is this?

'Is, uh, communing with nature something you do too?' I ask, my fingers nervously tapping against the tabletop.

'I used to, but then ...' Picking up a carton of ready-made custard, he snips open the top with kitchen scissors.

'Your penis got frostbite and fell off?' I say witheringly.

'No, I just don't anymore,' he replies cagily.

'Well, thank God.'

'Why?'

I lower my voice so no one else can hear. 'As your fake girlfriend, I may have been expected to do it too!'

'Oh no. We'd never make you do anything you weren't comfortable with.' Bailey grins at me, licking a dribble of custard off his finger. 'Well, not much.'

'What does that mean?'

But he doesn't reply as Kirk pipes up from over by the stove. 'What are you two lovebirds whispering about? Is the trifle finished?'

His comment brings Sasha and Susie over to the table. They ooh and aah at Bailey's creation. The pink berry, creamy yellow custard, and sponge extravaganza is finished off with dollops of whipped cream and sprinkles. Bailey has added sparklers round the edge and a few star cookies in the middle for good measure.

Hazel, who's left Charlie in the other room presumably to be babysat by Amy, puts her arm around his shoulder. 'It's lovely, Bails. Even better than last year.'

Kate comes to join in, with her boob thankfully now covered, and holds up her baby to see the dessert. 'Holly, meet Eve.' I shake her bootee foot, and she gurgles, then burps up a spattering of breast milk.

Suddenly, the back door flies open, and a blast of wintery air cuts through the kitchen like a knife. Jennifer, Allan, and Sarah come stomping in, along with another guy who I assume is Simon, the eldest. I brace myself, not knowing where to look. But they're all fully clothed, rugged up in winter coats and puffer jackets.

Sarah's cheeks are ruddy under her pink beanie, and she has a matching scarf. She stamps her feet on the back-door mat to get the snow off her boots. 'The sheep are OK, and the stream is still flowing in parts,' she says. 'I hope Mirabelle can make it through tomorrow. The snowbanks are getting high.'

She sees me staring at her open-mouthed. 'Are you catching flies, Holly?' she says in a teasing tone. I shut my mouth with a snap and look over at Bailey, who is rinsing dishes in the kitchen sink. His shoulders are heaving. He's just told me a load of old bollocks about his family being naturists just to shock me. Now he's laughing at my expense!

I clench my fists and say in a steely voice, 'Bailey, can I talk to you in private?'

He turns and quickly wipes away tears of mirth with the back of his hand.

'Oooh, lovers' quarrel,' drawls Kirk. He seems to be observing us rather closely, which is making me nervous. Maybe he's picking up on something not being quite right.

Bailey edges towards the kitchen door, and I stalk after him.

In the hallway, I'm about to let loose when he sprints upstairs, laughing like a hyena. I take off after him, trying to grab his jumper, but he's too quick.

Now I'm seeing red in all its glorious fury. He's going to pay for this. Bailey nips into his bedroom and tries to close the door in my face. But I manage to force it open, huffing and puffing, and we stumble into the room. Crumpet yelps and makes a dash for it out the door.

Before I know what's happening, Bailey's grabbed a

cushion and whacked me on the back with it, so I fall face down on the bed.

'Why, you little ...!' I growl.

I'm so mad I grab two cushions and start boxing him round the ears. He pummels me back, snickering in glee. I have to admit, it feels good to let out my anger about the TikTok, the Lewis betrayal, and Bailey himself for locking me into this situation.

One of my cushions splits, and a bunch of feathers swirl into the air, then start descending like soft snow. I discard the cushion as it starts losing impact and continue swinging wildly with the other one, managing to get in a few satisfying blows to his chest.

Feathers land on my cheeks, and I shake them off impatiently, intent on winning this fight. Bailey has feathers all over his hair. He looks like a plucked chicken, as, I suppose, do I.

We eye each other with our respective cushions held aloft, breathing hard. Then Bailey lowers his and holds out his hand.

'Truce? Before we rip my room to shreds?'

I look at his hand in silence. Deliberately, I ignore it and reach out and swiftly pluck the two beady eyes from his gingerbread man that have been glued on to his jumper. Running round to the sash window, I heave it up, chuck them out, and shut it again with a whump.

I stand there, panting—*take that.*

Bailey gives me a slow clap. 'Nice, veeeery mature.'

He goes over to his bag, unzips it, and pulls out another Christmas jumper—this one green. He takes off the red jumper intentionally slowly until he's in snug Levi's and a tight white T-shirt that hugs his bicep muscles. A flush of heat that has nothing to do with the recent exercise washes over me.

Bailey pulls on the other jumper just as deliberately slowly to annoy me. I'm now staring at a goofy Rudolph sporting a red nose and googly eyes.

I'm amused at his show of defiance. 'How many Christmas jumpers do you have in there?'

'More than enough to foil you. Bwahahaha.' He chuckles evilly.

'So I take it your family aren't naturists then? You fibber.'

'I think Mum did the odd bit of sunbathing in the garden when she was younger. But no, not as far as I'm aware. Your face when they walked in, though ...' He starts laughing again.

'Shut up.' But I can't help laughing a bit, and I feel lighter and more relaxed, as if thumping Bailey with a cushion has been cathartic in some way.

Chapter 9

After scooping up the feathers as best we can, Bailey tries to, unsuccessfully, stuff them back into the cushion.

'I'll sew it up at some point,' he says, poking the lumpy piece of fabric into the wardrobe.

'Sewing as well as cooking ... My, you are domestic,' I remark, attempting to comb out my tangled hair using my fingers. In the end, I give up and tie it back in a bushy ponytail.

From behind me, Bailey says, 'I think there's still a feather in there.'

He fiddles with my ponytail, and I bat his hand away. 'What are you doing?'

'Nothing.'

Downstairs, someone strikes a gong; and the resonant tone reverberates up the stairs, causing my spine to tingle.

'What the heck is that?' I ask, startled.

'Dinner,' says Bailey. 'The most efficient way of summoning the resident horde. We should go down, or we'll miss out.'

The dry sandwich I sampled on the train is a mere

memory and that pie smelled amazing. I'm famished.

As soon as we walk into the crowded dining room, Jennifer claps her hands together in delight. 'Oh, you two look so cute in your matching green!'

I'm wearing a white T-shirt, black cardigan, and jeans. So I'm not sure what 'green' she's referring to. I put my hand up to my ponytail and touch something springy. Bailey's attached the green tinsel bow to my hair. Grrrr! I almost take it out and fling it at him, but Kirk is watching us again. So I lower my hand and manage a passable smile.

Bailey slings an arm around my shoulder amicably. 'Green looks good on you, honey.'

I shrug it off when no one is watching.

'Don't call me 'honey',' I hiss at him, but he just chuckles. Soooo annoying. If he doesn't watch out, Rudolph's eyes will be joining the gingerbread man's in the snowdrifts.

I had visions of us all sitting round the dining table and making polite conversation by candlelight, but it doesn't quite turn out like that. I quickly learn that the dining table is nothing more than a cornucopia where the hunger games begin.

Bailey doesn't tell me the rules either. He simply hands me a plate from the pile, and I follow his lead, shyly observing the genial hubbub. Adults pass out cutlery and hand round condiments while kids whine that they don't like this or that. Some seem to be under the table. My foot keeps getting tapped by unseen hands.

Sarah locks eyes with me across the table and gives me an encouraging thumbs up while one of her blonde, blue-eyed twins complains about the brussels sprouts. 'Yes, you need to eat a few please, or there will be none of Uncle Bailey's special dessert.'

In this household, it appears that if you're late you miss out or if you're fussy you don't get pudding.

Once Bailey and I have helped ourselves from various serving dishes, I follow him into the substantial lounge. To my relief, the decorations in here are pared back. A log fire glows in the grate while the mantelpiece has a collection of Christmas cards arranged along the top and a row of small red Santa stockings dangle from inset hooks. It's all very warm, pleasant and inviting. No Christmas tree though, which is odd.

Family members sit in small breakout groups, either on sofas or cross-legged on the soft grey rug, tending to their children. It's like a yearly parent-child convention. Since we're childless, we join Jennifer and Allan, who've set up in a couple of armchairs in the far corner opposite an old piano. Bailey and I perch awkwardly on the piano bench with our plates in our laps.

At this point, I just want to eat, sleep, and slink off to Inverness tomorrow without any fuss. Whatever Bailey tells his parents about 'our relationship' when I've gone is up to him.

But Jennifer is intent on getting to know me.

'So, Holly,' she says, 'are your family originally from Scotland?'

She forks mashed potato into her mouth and chews slowly, waiting for my answer.

I swallow my mouthful of mushy peas. 'Uh, not really, just my grandmother. My parents live in Cornwall, and my sister lives in London.'

She pounces on this.

'Oh, lovely! Sarah and Mirabelle are in Bethnal Green. Where does your sister stay?'

'Putney.'

'Oh, right ... So why ...' Her forehead creases, and I can see what she's thinking: 'Why aren't you spending Christmas in London or Cornwall?' I sigh inwardly. Might as well tell her. I'm not going to see her again after tonight.

'They're my foster family, and we don't get on,' I say flatly. 'I'd rather spend Christmas with my biological grandmother.'

No one says anything, and I attempt to bridge the awkward silence with a flippant joke. 'You know what they say—you can choose your friends, but you can't choose your family, right?'

Jennifer leans forward like she's curious to hear more, but Allan shakes his head slightly at her, so she sits back and nods. 'Very true.' But I can tell she feels sorry for me. People normally do, which is why I don't tend to talk about it.

Time to change the subject. 'This pie is delicious, by the way.' It truly is. The flaky crust is buttery, and the steak and ale filling is warm melt-in-the-mouth goodness.

'You have Bailey to thank for that. He made it while you were having a nap. He brought the ale up from Edinburgh because he knows I like it,' says Allan.

'Along with a ham, a black pudding, several cheeses, berries, and bread,' contributes Jennifer.

'Gosh,' I say. 'He's like a travelling grocer.'

But Bailey doesn't react to my subtle dig. He's got his head down and is ploughing steadily through his food without looking at me. I can't tell what he's thinking. His quietness makes me feel vulnerable at having shared that family snippet. But when he comes up for air, he rests his arm against mine briefly, and I feel a bit relieved that he's not treating me like a pariah. Though I suppose if we were actually dating, he'd probably know about my history, so he can't exactly overreact in front of his parents.

Jennifer has moved on and, under the impression that I know their last name, is telling me about their family tartan.

'It's similar to the Keighley, but it's got a bolder streak of red. You might've seen Bailey's couch cushions at his flat?'

I nod sagely, as if I've been there. I don't even know where he lives. 'Oh, yes, that's a lovely one. Very, er, Christmassy,' I say, taking a stab in the dark that if Bailey's involved, it will be festive.

Jennifer smiles. 'Yes, it is! That's why I thought he'd like them. Such a rich shade of green too.'

Right, green-and-red tartan—that narrows it down.

'You may have also heard of our famous distant cousin,' says Bailey, and I assume he's trying to help me out. 'The Hollywood actress. She was in that movie with Ryan Gosling.'

I stare at him blankly. Emma Stone from *Crazy, Stupid, Love*? But that's not a Scottish name.

'Also the one about time travel,' he prompts. Then it clicks. Luckily, I'm a fan. Otherwise, this could get painful.

'Oh, Rachel McAdams!'

I hear Bailey puff out a sigh of relief, and Jennifer beams. 'Yes! We haven't actually met her, but I believe she has a strong connection to this area.'

'Either that, or she likes whisky,' quips Allan.

I feel like doing a victory punch. Their last name is

McAdams. We're getting somewhere!

After the main course, there's a cry of 'Pudding!' from one of the kids. This results in a general stampede towards the dining room table. Bailey and I join the back of the crowd. I'm curious as to what all the fuss is about. His sisters have cleared away dinner and strewn the white tablecloth with silver sequins, and there's a whole range of desserts nestling on top: strawberries cut in half and joined with frosting to resemble mini Santas (complete with eyes and jacket buttons), scoops of vanilla ice cream with sprinkles and sparklers, red velvet cupcakes with chocolate reindeer antlers, gingerbread star cookies with snowflake icing decorations.

My eyes widen. It's a festive sugar overload. Bailey is surveying the table with a pleased look on his face. 'Did you do all this?' I ask him.

'Yes, while you were napping. Hazel and Kirk helped.'

'I did some icing too!' exclaims Susie, jumping up and down so emphatically her fluffy pink hairband flops down over her eyes.

'Yes, you did,' says Bailey, gently adjusting it for her. He holds her hand, as if to stop her from excitedly springing onto the table.

Jennifer comes out through the swinging door with Bailey's sparkler trifle aloft and deposits it on the table, where it proudly takes centre stage. Everyone oohs and claps.

'I thought the trifle was for Christmas?' I say to him, surprised.

'Nah, this is just the pre-Christmas line-up, to celebrate everyone being here.'

I nod, feeling a bit overwhelmed. I shouldn't be surprised—Bailey's over the top when it comes to Christmas, and so is his whole family, it seems.

'Bails, do you want to do the honours?' asks Sarah, holding out a clickable fire starter.

'It's all right. You can. I'll keep Holly company. Make sure she doesn't steal any cookies for a midnight feast.'

Susie giggles at that.

A hush falls as someone kills the lights, and it's like a ceremonial ritual is about to take place. Sarah lights the sparklers, and the kids' faces lined up round the table are illuminated by the bright fizz like miniature cherubs.

Then the lights are back on, and everyone's digging in. Bailey goes off to help serve.

'Bailey is an amazing cook, but you probably already know that. Wait 'til you try his Christmas pudding. It's a whisky flambé,' says Hazel conversationally, waiting for the initial rush to subside.

'Ah, I won't be here, more's the pity,' I reply. I knew

there would have to be alcohol involved at some point. Last night's session at the hotel is all too fresh. I'm still feeling seedy. I'm going to swear off drinking. Forever.

'Oh, sorry. I forgot you're heading to your grandmother's tomorrow. You can take something with you. Bails won't mind.'

I look over at Bailey, who's serving dollops of trifle. He happens to glance over at me, and we lock eyes for a moment. Discomforted again by the intensity in his gaze, I look away first. Something feels different between us, but I can't figure out what.

'There's always loads,' continues Hazel. 'Everyone usually rolls home after the holidays, having gained half a stone.'

I feel like saying something about the evils of sugar, but it feels churlish when everyone's so excited. I bite my tongue.

Bailey comes over to me. 'What would you like?'

'Uh, I'm not much of a dessert person.'

But my protest goes unheard. Soon, he's back with a full plate of goodies, then disappears again.

I nibble on the edge of a gingerbread star cookie silently in the corner. A strong need to escape washes over me, and I back away towards the door, hoping that Bailey is too busy to notice. But he catches me before I can go through it.

'Where are you going?' he asks.

I hand him my plate. 'I'm feeling really tired. I might turn in. Sorry.'

I keep my head down as I walk away so I don't have to see any disappointment or pity on his face.

Chapter 10

I'm in my PJs on my side of the cushion barrier, attempting to fall asleep, when Bailey bounds into the room. The wardrobe door bangs, and then he kicks the edge of the bed and squawks.

'Do you mind? You'll wake Crumpet.' He's been loaned Rupert's old dog bed and is snoring softly in the corner of the room.

'Sorry, it's dark. I can't see what I'm doing.'

'It's not that dark. There's a full moon. Maybe you need glasses.' Thankfully someone has turned off the Christmas lights outside otherwise it would be like a disco in here.

'I won't be a minute.' Bailey leaves again, I assume to use the bathroom. This is going to be a loooong night.

Wide awake now, I sit up and unlock my phone. I've been studiously avoiding it ever since the message from TikTok admin at Kingussie station. But I'm surprised to discover that Andrea has sent a text wishing me a 'Merry Xmas' and hoping that I'm OK. Nice to know someone cares if I live or die. I send her a quick reply, leaving out any details of where I am, except that I'm safe. The fact that I'm in Bailey's bed isn't something I want to share, even if it's a perfectly innocent scenario.

Bailey enters, and I flip my phone face down on my chest. His shadow lurches across the curtains like a werewolf in a horror film. There's a rustle of clothing being removed. Then the bed dips as he gets in the other side.

Cautiously, I lift my phone and place it on the nightstand. Bailey is now quiet and unmoving, but I can hear his breathing. It's disturbingly loud.

I close my eyes and wait for sleep to come, but I'm not used to sleeping with someone right next to me, even behind a wall of cushions. Neither, it appears, is Bailey.

'Are you asleep?' he stage-whispers.

'Not really.'

'So what's going on with you?'

'Nothing.'

'But you took off in a hurry during dessert.'

'I'm fine. It's just been a long day,' I reply bluntly. But Bailey isn't easily dissuaded.

'It's just ...'

'What?'

'That stuff you said about being fostered.'

My emotional guard dogs are immediately on high alert. 'What about it?'

'It can't have been easy for you.'

I shift position under the bedclothes. 'I guess. I don't know anything else, though, do I?'

'Is Christmas that bad with your ... foster family?'

'Let's just say it's not like here. The last time I had Christmas with them was two years ago. I vowed I'd never do it again.' It actually took me a month to recover mentally from the experience.

'What happened?' Bailey's voice softens imperceptibly.

'A lot of arguing mostly. It's usually about money, not having enough. Violet, my foster sister, is a "glass half-empty" person. There's typically some drama about things that aren't going well in her life. She gets it from her mother. The two of them together are ... trying.'

'And your foster father?'

'A hypochondriac—he's always talking about how he's got some incurable illness. Believe me, after two days of listening to them all, I'm ready to come home.'

Bailey gives a sympathetic grunt. 'Is there a tree, decorations, or presents at least?'

'No to all three. They think Christmas is nothing but commercialist shite. They invite me out of obligation. We usually go out to a restaurant.'

'So you've never really had a proper Christmas?'

'Not really, not like in the movies at least.'

'What age were you when you went to live with them?'

'When I was 8. I was supposed to be company for Violet. I managed to get on OK with her then, but now she's so moody it's like trying to converse with the Grim Reaper.'

There's a long silence from Bailey's side of the bed. He doesn't ask any more questions, probably sensing he's getting into painful territory. Then the cushions move aside next to my arm, and something warm touches my hand. I let out a yelp.

'It's just me,' he says, grabbing hold of my fingers.

My breath catches in my throat, and my stomach flips. 'What are you doing?'

'What does it look like?'

His palm is warm, dry, and smooth against mine. It actually feels really nice, but alarm bells are ringing in my brain as I try to comprehend what it means. A friendly gesture? A come-on? We are in the same bed. But I don't find Bailey attractive in the slightest. He's the most annoying guy I've ever met.

'I'm just ... I'm here if you ever want to talk about anything.' He squeezes my hand gently, and self-piteous tears prick my eyeballs. *Ah, OK, he's feeling sorry for the foster kid because she missed out on Christmas.*

I disentangle my fingers from his because it's suddenly unbearable to have him touching me. I wish I'd never said anything about my family situation.

'Sorry, I know you're trying to be nice to me, but I can't,' I mumble.

Bailey doesn't seem put out. 'It's good that you made contact with your grandmother at least,' he says, stifling a yawn. 'Is that a recent thing?'

'Er, yes. When I moved to Edinburgh, I looked into my family history.' That part isn't really true. The English grandmother is alive and kicking, the old boot. But the Scottish grandmother is mythical. However, I'd like to think that if she did exist, she would've been overjoyed to have me visit for Christmas.

Bailey's warm hand is still resting beside mine. He hasn't retracted it back through the cushion barrier. All I have to do is reach out and take it. I inch my fingers forward, but I can't make myself—not after I said I couldn't.

'We'd better get some sleep, I guess,' he says.

He withdraws his hand back through the cushions, and I feel somewhat relieved.

'If I snore, just throw a cushion at me,' he says sleepily.

'If you snore, I'll whack you with it.'

Bailey chuckles and rolls over. 'I know you will.'

When I wake to a pale light filtering through the curtains, Bailey isn't there, and neither is Crumpet. He must've taken him down to the kitchen to feed him. I stretch and luxuriate in the feeling of being blessedly alone. Despite everything that happened yesterday and a strange man beside me, I slept pretty well. But I guess Bailey technically isn't so much of a stranger anymore.

My eyes flick to the corkboard on the wall. Maybe since we're sharing our troubled pasts, he'll tell me what happened with that girl—not that I'm dying to know or anything, just curious.

Eventually, I get up and don a fresh pair of jeans and top and my usual black cardigan. My hair refuses to behave itself, and I don't really want to wash it, so I tie it back again. The tinsel bow is lying on the nightstand, but I leave it there. I'm not a girl who wears tinsel, even if Bailey is trying to coerce me into being one.

I head to the kitchen, thinking Bailey will be there alone, only to discover him sitting at the table, bouncing Charlie on his knee. Across from him, Hazel has a cup of tea in one hand and a piece of toast in the other. Kirk isn't there, thank goodness. I can do without his astute gaze on me this early in the morning.

Bailey looks up when I walk in and grins. 'Och, Charlie, it's a Christmas miracle! She's never up before nine on a holiday.'

Hazel smiles at me. She's wearing flowery pyjama bottoms and a chunky orange sweater with a hole in the elbow. 'Morning, Holly. Help yourself to anything you like.'

'Morning,' I reply, surveying the table, which is laid with a big brown teapot, cereal boxes, a jug of milk, and a bowl of fruit. There's also fresh bread and assorted spreads. My stomach rumbles as I take a seat.

'Bailey was going to do a fry-up, but he's being lazy,' Hazel admonishes.

'Not my fault. I didn't get to sleep until late,' he says and winks at me.

I reach for a cereal box, feeling mightily self-conscious after our 'chat' last night. Trust him to make it sound like we 'slept' together to keep up the pretence—as if I'd agree to *that* in his parents' house, ugh.

'Where's Crumpet?' I ask, changing the subject before Bailey can spout any more innuendos.

'I think he's outside with Sarah and the girls. They went to get some fresh air,' says Hazel.

Hmm, I'm not sure I like everyone bonding with Crumpet so much. It's not like they're ever going to see him again.

Sure enough, they all come bursting into the kitchen five minutes later, along with an elegant slim woman with short dark hair wearing a grey belted coat. Crumpet bounds in behind them, buoyed up by their energy.

'Look who we found!' exclaims Sarah, smiling widely

and flinging off her mittens. The twins yell 'Mumma's here!' before anyone has a chance to say anything. Ahh, I take it this is Mirabelle.

There's a flurry of everyone hugging. I get introduced and given two cheek kisses. It turns out she spent the night in Dundee and then set off at six this morning due to the forecast.

'They were talking about a big dumping around lunchtime, so I didn't want to get caught. Imagine spending a snowy Christmas in Dundee by myself!' Mirabelle gives a tinkling laugh, and the others sympathise with what-ifs and 'How awful!'

Since this is exactly what I'm facing in Inverness, I don't join in the merriment.

Bailey nudges my shoulder. 'We should probably get going soon if that's the case. I don't want to be too late back as I need to start prepping dinner.'

I rouse from my fog of gloom. 'Oh, right. Yes. I'll get my things together.'

Trudging back upstairs with Crumpet and an apple for the road, I leave behind the chatter and warmth of the kitchen. Looks like I'm going to Inverness sooner than expected. I thought I might at least get the morning to relax, but Bailey's shipping me out. I know it's not the case—it's because of the impending snow forecast. But it feels a bit like he's getting rid of me. I feel irrationally hurt, which is ridiculous. Why would he want me here when all I do is make sarcastic remarks and bring him down with my woeful stories of Christmases past? It's better I leave now. If we had another night in his bed together, who knows what I'd end up telling him!

Stuffing clothes and toiletries into my bag, I make sure Crumpet has his lead and toys.

'Time to go, mate.'

If there's anyone I feel sorry for, it's Crumpet. He genuinely seemed to enjoy making friends with the McAdams family. Now all he's got to look forward to is me, a dowdy room with a single-bar heater, and bit of bacon for breakfast (if he's lucky).

While Bailey warms up the Range Rover in the adjacent garage, the entire family dons coats and hats and comes out to see us off from the front stoop. They say it's to get some fresh air and for the kids to burn off some energy, so I gather it's not entirely about me.

After saying goodbye, Kirk and his kids (the young girl I saw reading on the windowsill yesterday and a gangly pre-teen boy) stomp off through the snow with a sled and a couple of bin lids to find a slope. Crumpet strains at his lead. He loves playing in the snow. The sky hangs low and grey against the treeline.

'Brrrr, it's freezing,' comments Sarah, rubbing her arms. 'There's definitely more snow coming. I hope Bails makes it back OK.'

'Where's Aunty Holly going?' asks Sasha. *Yikes, now I'm their aunty.*

'Aunty Holly is spending Christmas in Inverness with her grannie,' explains Sarah.

'But what about the tree?' pipes up Susie.

'She'll have her own tree.'

Susie pouts. 'I bet it's not like ours. It's so fun, and there's hot chocolate and marshmallows.'

Seeing I'm clueless, Sarah explains, 'We have a tree-trimming ceremony on Christmas Eve. Everyone helps decorate it. Ready for *Santa*.' She raises her eyebrows at me.

'Ah!' I reply, thinking, *I'm glad I won't be here for all that palaver!*

As the Range Rover comes into view, she sniffs and says, 'Right. I hate goodbyes, so merry Christmas and all that. You and Bails can come and visit us in London now we know you exist.'

I gulp.

Feeling like a stiff-limbed manikin being passed around, I'm hugged and patted on the back with a chorus of 'Lovely to meet you' and 'We'll see you again'.

Then Crumpet jumps into the back seat, and I'm bundled into the front, and everyone's waving merrily as we drive off. What a performance! So much for slinking away quietly.

Chapter 11

I touch the foil-wrapped package resting on my knees and take a deep breath. Jennifer handed it to me at the last minute.

'A few Christmas cookies for you and your grannie to have with a cup of tea,' she said before giving me a tight hug.

That was the worst part. I feel like a right cow for deceiving her, and it's all Bailey's fault.

'You're a proper gobshite,' I mutter. I'm royally ticked off at him and more than a little apprehensive about spending the rest of my holiday in a cold Inverness guest house.

'Huh?' He shifts his eyes briefly from the road to me.

'If you'd just said I was a work colleague or something, your mum wouldn't be treating me like a potential daughter-in-law.'

Bailey tightens his grip on the steering wheel—oooh, I'm getting to him! Good! Then he relaxes them. 'We've been through this. If I had, you'd be sitting here complaining about being woken up at 5 a.m. from screaming kids. I did it for you and my own sanity so I didn't have to listen to you berate me.'

I huff in consternation. 'The kids seemed well behaved to me. I didn't hear any screaming this morning.'

'That's because you were sound asleep, and yes, I checked. Trust me, the screaming happened. I got up at 6 a.m. and took Crumpet outside for a walk to give my ears a rest.'

Even weirder than Bailey walking my dog is that he saw me sleeping. 'Was I drooling?'

He chuckles. 'No, but you were making this bizarre face.'

'What face?'

He screws up his nose and mouth until he looks half demented.

I whack his shoulder. 'I do not do that!'

He relaxes his features back to normal. 'How do you know if you're asleep? All I can say is, you looked like you wanted to kill someone, so I got out of there quickly.'

'What a load of rubbish. And don't change the subject.'

Bailey sighs. 'Look, if it means that much to you, I'll tell them as soon as I get back.'

'Good. And make sure they know it was your idea, not mine!'

He nods.

We fall into a tense silence for the next half an hour. I

stare, unseeing, at the snow-covered fields whisking by. Now that I'm not arguing with Bailey, I can't ignore the fact that soon I'm going to be alone—with nothing between me and the TikTok. It's been growing exponentially. I know it has. By now, millions of people all over the world have seen my anti-Christmas rant. Shame rattles my gut, and I let out a small groan of despair, causing Bailey to look over.

'Did you say something?'

I clear my throat. 'No, I didn't.'

I'm sorely tempted to tell Bailey about the TikTok and get his opinion on what his 'friend' Lewis has done to me. But I'm not sure how close they are or if he'll even think I've been wronged. Knowing Bailey, he'll probably think it's just deserts because I dissed his sacred holiday. Maybe I should turn the spotlight on him for a change?

'Actually, I was wondering ... That corkboard in your room with the photos ...'

'What about it?' He doesn't sound wary or defensive, so I plough on.

'Was that you with your ex-girlfriend?'

'Yes, Rosalie. It was about two years ago.' He rubs his nose briefly. I know I shouldn't pry, but now I've started, I can't stop.

'What happened?'

Bailey beeps the horn, startling me. But it's just to warn a hawk pecking at roadkill, and it flies skyward. After we've driven over the flattened furry mess, he says, 'She got together with someone else ... while she was still with me. One of the guys from that camping trip actually.'

I wince. 'Ouch, sorry.'

He straightens his shoulders and doesn't look at me. 'It was a hard thing to go through, but I'm over it now.'

'Why keep those photos then? Isn't it like rubbing lemon juice in the wound every time you look at them? I'd have ripped them to shreds!'

'That trip isn't a painful memory. It's a happy one. Why should I destroy my happy memory just because of what she did? It would be like cutting off my nose to spite my face.'

I don't really understand that way of thinking.

'If you say so, but I still think it's masochistic. If someone did something that hurtful to me, I'd rather not be reminded of them.'

'I don't think it's masochistic in the slightest. That's a bit extreme,' says Bailey stubbornly.

'Can you see my point of view at all?'

'Not really.'

Aargh. He's so bloody annoying. I check Google Maps on my phone. Ten minutes until we get to Inverness, thank God. I'm glad I won't have to see him again. He really knows how to push my buttons. I'm sorry I asked about his stupid corkboard. Why the hell would he want to keep photos of his ex who cheated on him? Unless he's still in love with her?

When we're on the outskirts of Inverness, I realise that, without thinking, I've given Bailey the address of the guest house to punch into the satnav. It's going to look mighty strange that my 'grandmother' is living at the Cumberfeldy Inn.

As we turn into the street, I panic. 'You can just drop me off here,' I say. 'Crumpet needs a toilet stop, and we can walk the rest of the way.' Phew, Crumpet always comes in handy if I need an excuse.

Bailey obediently pulls over, and I open the car door. 'Leave the biscuits and your bag in the car if that's easier,' he says. 'I'll just follow you to the house.'

'Er, that's OK. No need,' I reply. 'You'd best be off in case it starts snowing.'

'The footpath's icy, though. You don't want your leg in a cast for Christmas.'

'I'm sure I'll be fine, but thanks, Mum.' I grab my bag from the boot, unzip the top, and stuff the biscuits in.

Crumpet jumps out when I open the back door of the car, and I call through to Bailey, 'Thanks for the lift and for putting me up for the night!'

'No problem. Have a good Christmas!' He lifts a hand in

farewell.

'You too.' I slam the door, a little harder than I mean to. OK, so he didn't ask to exchange numbers. But really, why did I expect that?

Crumpet, fed up with waiting for me, trots off down the footpath. I drag my bag, walking as fast as I dare after him. 'Crumpet! Come back here!' Why is he being so disobedient now of all moments? One of my heels skids from under me, and I nearly go flying.

Next thing I know, Bailey has exited the car and is chasing after Crumpet. He manages to catch up to him when he stops to pee on a gatepost.

'Maybe it's best if I walk with you to the house.'

Silently, I hand him Crumpet's lead, and he clips it on. 'Is it this way?'

I nod. Inside, I'm freaking out. But what can I do? Go up to a random person's house? Knock on their door and pretend I'm related?

We proceed down the street until we're outside the guest house. Oh god.

Luckily, it looks like a normal brick semi-detached house. It has a small front garden and a low wrought-iron fence with a gate. Maybe if I'm quick about it, Bailey won't notice anything—like the small white sign with blue lettering saying 'Cumberfeldy Inn'.

'This is me,' I say, taking Crumpet's lead out of his hand. I open the gate to go in, but Bailey isn't moving.

'Your grandmother lives at the Cumberfeldy Inn?' he asks, sounding bemused. Shit. He's spotted the sign.

'Er, yes. It's like a guest house slash retirement home. She's been living here for years.' I bite my lip, knowing if I say any more, it's going to sound like a blatant lie. Bailey stares at me for a moment and frowns. *Just go*, I beg silently.

'Well, I guess I'll see you around, Holly,' he says. 'Merry Christmas again.' He looks like he wants to say something else but doesn't.

'Merry Christmas. Drive safely.' I hustle up the path to the front door, risking a peek to see if he's gone. Yes! Bailey is wandering back to the Range Rover. It looks like he's taken the bait. I heave a sigh of relief. 'That was close, buddy,' I say to Crumpet. 'But I think we got away with it.'

The reception is unmanned, so I ding the bell on the counter. The room is wood panelled with stone beams running along the top. There's a stale smell of lingering cabbage overladen with Febreze. The door swings open, and a man with thinning hair comes lumbering through. I gather he's the cheerful soul I spoke to on the phone. He's wearing a grey shirt with the sleeves rolled up and a tweed vest. From his greasy lips, I gather I've interrupted a late breakfast or early lunch.

'Yes?'

'Um, I'm Holly Driver. I was supposed to check in yesterday, but I had train issues.'

He harrumphs and taps on an ancient laptop. 'You're lucky I didn't give yer room away. It's a busy time of year, and we're full up.' I haven't yet seen a single person, so I can't judge the accuracy of this statement. I'll have to take his word for it. 'So yer booked for four nights, and yer checking out on Wednesday?'

I nod. Crumpet scratches his belly with his hind paw, and the man leans over the desk. 'Och, you have a dawg.'

'Yes, he's quiet and clean.'

The man harrumphs again. 'I suppose that's OK.'

'Well, yes, I did check with you on the phone, and you said it was.' The man's jaw tightens, but he doesn't say anything. Somehow, I don't think we're going to be pals. He fishes under the counter and hands me a laminated typed menu that looks like it's been around since the 1970s. 'Just tae let yer know, I'm doing a bit o' grub on Christmas Day. Lunch only.'

There are three courses, and nothing looks particularly appetising. The thought of gnawing on dry turkey and spooning up soggy vegetables isn't appealing. Ugh. I feel a sudden pang at the thought of missing out on the

McAdamses' Christmas dinner. Even though he annoys the heck out of me, I grudgingly admit that Bailey is a great cook.

I hand the menu back. 'I think I'll pass, thanks.'

'Suit yerself. Breakfast is at 7.30 sharp. If yer not in the dining room by then, I won't bother cooking yer bacon and beans.'

I sigh inwardly, collect the key the man hands me, and, following his pointed finger, trundle off along a corridor.

I'm hoping that the room is better than I remembered, but it's not. It's worse than the photos. I stand in the doorway and gaze around in horror. There's a suspect rusty brown stain on the carpet by the window that could be either blood or poop—take your pick. One end of the curtain is falling off the rail. There are long rips in the wallpaper like someone staying here couldn't handle it and went insane. The beige pillows on the single bed are even flatter than in the photos, if that's possible. The smell of Febreze is overpowering, and I'm worried that when it lifts, an even worse stench than cabbage will be detected.

Crumpet takes a step into the room, whines, and looks up at me. His brown eyes are questioning why the heck I brought him here when he was having a lovely time at the McAdamses'. I'm starting to wonder that myself.

Maybe the bathroom isn't too bad. If it has a nice

bathtub, at least I can have a soak. I push the inner door open, and it swings back to reveal tired brown-tiled decor from the middle of the last century. Gingerly, I lift the wooden toilet seat. It's old and stained, but thankfully, nothing's bobbing in there. The bath tap, when I turn it, shudders and groans. But no water comes out. There's a separate shower that stinks of bleach. Lord. So much for a relaxing Christmas getaway to escape my demons. It feels like they're all congregating in this guest house. In a few hours, it will be dark, and I'll be at their mercy. I switch on the bedside lamp, and the bulb blows.

It's the last straw of an extremely trying few days, and I can feel myself starting to unravel. I walk around, flapping my hands at my face and deep breathing, but I can't hold it back. A flood of tears erupts; and soon, I'm bawling like a baby, eyes and nose streaming. Even more than the TikTok or the hideous guest house I'm now in, I'm vaguely aware that Bailey leaving and not asking for my number hurt me more than I care to admit. *You stupid idiot*, I berate myself. *He was really kind to you, and all you did was act like a cow. At this point, he's driving back to Ballindalloch feeling relieved he never has to see you again. And you ruined his cushion.* Thinking of him sewing it up and hating me makes me cry even harder.

I lean against the wall and wipe my face with my sleeve,

pushing thoughts of Bailey in his tight white T-shirt out of my mind, while Crumpet whines and paws my jeans. 'It's OK, buddy. I'm OK,' I say, trying to reassure him. But I know I'm really not OK. My life is held together with tenuous threads, and if one starts fraying, the whole lot could unravel. If I'm not careful, I could end up tearing bits of wallpaper off like my previous fellow guest. Taking a deep shuddering breath, I head into the bathroom to find something on which to blow my nose. There's one toilet roll, half used. A small victory.

When I come back, Crumpet is by the window, looking at something in the garden. He gives a low growl. Probably seen a rabbit. I go over and peer out, and a figure in a dark coat suddenly appears in front of the window, and I let out a scream. Crumpet leaps up excitedly. Oh god, it gets worse. Does the guest house manager perv through the windows? The figure turns to face me, and then I realise—I know those googly eyes.

Chapter 12

Heaving up the sash window, I poke my head out into the icy air. 'What the fuck? You scared me half to death!'

Bailey pulls a contrite face. 'Uh, sorry. I wasn't sure which room was yours. Then I saw Crumpet. Can I come in? It's freezing out here.' He jigs around on the frozen ground, crushing plants underfoot.

I step back, and Bailey awkwardly folds himself under the lip of the window. He slides forward on the sill and tumbles through onto the carpet, narrowly missing the stain.

After he's in, I yank down the window sharply, shutting off the flow of cold air and turn on him. 'Why the hell are you lurking around in the garden?' My relief at seeing him makes the words come out sharper than I intended. Crumpet whines at my tone.

Bailey gets up and brushes off his coat while Crumpet bounces around him. He rubs his head. 'Hey, boy. I tried reception, but that guy refused to let me see you. Grumpy bastard, what's with him?'

I agree. But because I'm perverse, I stick up for the grumpy bastard. 'He's just making sure guests aren't harassed.'

Bailey raises his eyebrows, and I fold my arms defensively. 'Well?' I ask, resisting the urge to tap my foot.

'Something wasn't sitting right about you being here. Then I thought maybe "I'm visiting my grandmother" was a euphemism for "I'm escaping my abusive boyfriend".'

His gaze shifts to my red, watery eyes and the crumpled piece of toilet paper I'm still clutching in my fist.

'I'm right, aren't I? You're on the run from some jerk.'

I quickly stuff the toilet paper into my pocket out of sight.

'There's no abusive boyfriend.'

'Then why are you crying?'

'I ... I just have a cold.'

Bailey looks disbelieving. He strides to the wardrobe and yanks it open, then does the same with the bathroom door. 'Just as I thought—no sweet little old grannie. I think you'd better spill the beans about why you're choosing to stay in this ...' He eyes the ripped wallpaper and wrinkles his snub nose. 'Shitty hole for Christmas.'

'It's a long story.'

He sits on the bed, making the springs creak alarmingly, and crosses his legs at the ankles. He pats the space beside him. 'I've got time.'

I hesitate. Should I tell him? On one hand, it would be a

relief. But he'll want to see the TikTok, and I'm ashamed of my anti-festive rant. Bailey is so pro-Christmas that he might be disgusted, and I realise that I don't want that. I want him to like me, even if it's only a smidgeon.

Feeling like I'm going to my execution, I perch next to him on the bed, being careful not to bump elbows. Crumpet flops by my feet and heaves a sigh, as if to say 'Here we go'.

'I couldn't stand to be in my flat for Christmas. It felt like the walls were closing in on me ...' I say in a faltering voice.

'Go on,' Bailey says in an encouraging tone.

'So ... I decided to go to Inverness for a bit. I thought I'd book somewhere to stay en route, but all the guest houses were full apart from this place. Then the train broke down, and I met you ... And you were asking all these questions. I didn't want to admit I was alone for Christmas like a loser. So yes, I fibbed about my grandmother.'

Bailey silently digests this.

Please let him believe me. It's partly the truth, the watered-down version.

'Do you really want to stay here?' he asks slowly.

I shake my head. 'Not particularly.'

'Then I think you should come back to the house with me. This place is dire.' He looks at the stain on the carpet. 'I think someone's bled to death over there.'

I breathe out in relief. 'If that's still an option, thanks. But one question.'

'What?'

'Why are you doing this? Helping me out, I mean. I'm a Christmas killjoy.'

'Maybe I'm hoping the McAdams family will change your mind about that.' He places an arm around my shoulder and gives it a friendly squeeze. 'Let's go, this place stinks of cabbage.'

Bailey meets me outside after I deal with Mr Grumpy Bastard, whose face went puce when I told him I wasn't staying after all.

'How did it go?' he asks, putting my bag in the boot.

'Let's just say he wasn't happy about it.'

I paid him for last night, but I said the room was a tip and refused to pay for another three nights or for the bloody beans and bacon, which he was entirely obsessed about. I'm just glad I'm out of there, and Crumpet seems to have cheered up too. When we drive off, I twist around to check; and he's sitting on the back seat, looking perkily out the window.

We've hardly left Inverness when the first flakes start falling. Bailey flicks on the windscreen wipers and peers up at the darkening sky. 'We should be all right, as long as it doesn't get too heavy.'

There's something magical about driving through snow, especially when you're inside a warm car. Bailey puts on the radio and searches for a station with Christmas carols. I assume he's determined to get me in a festive mood. But Bailey humming along with 'Hark! The Herald Angels Sing' doesn't set my teeth on edge like it normally would. Maybe it has something to do with the way his hand is tapping precariously close to mine on the gearstick. I'm not sure what's going on, why all the animosity I had towards him has disappeared. In its place is something resembling ... gratitude.

I clear my throat. 'Thanks again for this.'

Bailey doesn't take his eyes from the road. 'You're welcome.' He smiles, as if he knows I'm watching him, and a dimple appears in his smooth cheek. My heart flutters like a bird in a cage. I grip the door handle tightly to ground myself. What the hell? Bailey's dimples are *not* that cute. I force myself to think practically.

'So we should get our story straight.'

Bailey inclines his head in my direction. 'What story?'

'Er, me not staying at the guest house? Your family is going to want to know why.'

'Hmm, I guess they will.'

'We could just tell them the truth—that we met randomly at a Christmas party two days ago. We bumped into each other at the train station, and you offered me a place to stay for the night. It doesn't explain why I'm now not in Inverness, though. I don't really want to get into details about why I invented my grandmother even though they sort of know about my family situation.'

Bailey is silent for a bit. 'Maybe we don't need to tell them anything,' he offers cautiously.

'What? We have to say something. It's going to be awkward enough when I turn up again after everyone waved me off—"Oh, look, here's Holly back again, with her dog and gingerbread biscuits".'

'Just leave it with me. I'll think of something. It'll be OK.'

I'm not happy about it, but he knows his family better than I do. Sensing my reluctance, Bailey takes my hand and rubs his thumb gently over my knuckles. 'Would it be awful being my girlfriend for a couple more days?'

A warm glow settles over me, melting some of the pack ice around my heart. His touch is disconcertingly nice, but I force myself to move my hand away. 'If it means I get a decent meal and a good night's sleep, I can pretend to be anyone's girlfriend.'

Bailey chuckles. 'That's the spirit. Oh, I love this one!' He turns up the volume, and 'Snoopy's Christmas' floods my ears. I take a deep breath and stare at the snow, now coming down in thick flurries.

Fuck. Somehow, I seem to have developed a slight hero worship crush on Bailey, thanks to him rescuing me from the guest house. Now I have to pretend to be his fake girlfriend when there's a part of me that's wishing I was his real one. And he's completely unaware of how he's affecting me. I thought his family home would be a safe haven for the next few days, but now I see I'm about to get entangled emotionally—something I don't need in my already-complicated life.

Panic rears up in my chest like a frightened colt. *I can't do this.*

But I have no choice, unless I open the door right now and fling myself out onto a snowdrift. And knowing Bailey, he'd simply pick me up, dust me off, and bundle me back in the car, then continue cheerfully on his way towards Ballindalloch—much like he's doing now, singing along with the Royal Guardsmen at the top of his lungs, 'Christmas bells, those Christmas bells, ringing through the land!'

Chapter 13

'Holly, yay!' Susie and Sasha rush to hug me round the legs, and I pat their heads awkwardly. I feel exhausted after the two-hour round trip, but we've finally arrived back. Everyone crowds around us in the kitchen, astonishment on their faces, talking all at once.

'What happened?'

'Couldn't you get through?'

'I thought that might happen. Mirabelle was lucky.'

'Did you get hold of your grannie?'

I nod to all the questions, not knowing what to say. Bailey goes along with the general assumption that the weather is the reason we're back.

'The weather got worse farther north, so we decided to turn around. Better to be safe than sorry. And now Holly gets to spend Christmas with us, which I'm glad about,' he says meaningfully. His serious tone makes me want to laugh. It almost sounds like he means it.

I notice Kirk's eyes on us, so I slide my hand into Bailey's like I suppose a real girlfriend would. He looks down in surprise but doesn't flinch. He laces his fingers through mine, and my stomach hops.

'I bet you are,' says Jennifer, smiling fondly at us holding hands. Her eyes have that glazed look, as if she's picturing me walking down the aisle in white tulle.

'Me too. Now you can help us with the treeeee!' Susie exclaims in a sing-song voice, and everyone laughs.

'Well, we'd better take Holly's bag back up to my room again,' Bailey announces.

'Yes, then come down and have some lunch,' says Jennifer. 'You must be starving. Allan's made a big pot of leek and potato soup, and there's some crusty bread to go with it.'

My stomach growls in anticipation. I'm so hungry I could eat the whole pot myself. Whatever happens with Bailey, I am so glad to be back in this house, where there's food, warmth, and fun.

Crumpet is scooped up by Sarah, who seems to have taken a real shine to him. 'You can leave this one here,' she says, and I nod. He seems happy enough with her.

In his room, Bailey dumps my wheelie. 'Well, that went smoothly,' he says. 'We didn't actually even have to lie.'

'Your brother Kirk is onto us. He keeps watching me, like he doesn't believe we're together,' I reply sceptically.

'Well, we'll just have to be better actors.'

'What does that entail?'

He shrugs. 'Och, I dunno ... more cuddly? There's usually some mistletoe around. Maybe we can stand under that?'

My cheeks heat, and my heart thumps. 'I'm not going to kiss you in front of everyone!' I splutter.

Bailey looks amused. 'Calm down. I was only joking.'

'Oh.' So this is all just a big laugh to him ...?

'Though it might look weird if we aren't more touchy-feely,' he muses. 'It is supposed to be a new relationship after all, and that's usually the period when people can't keep their hands off each other.'

I swallow hard ... Or maybe not?

The gong sounds from the bowels of the house.

'Time for lunch,' says Bailey. He sees my anxious expression and smirks. 'Don't worry, I'll try not to grope you in public.'

'Grope me, and you die!' I growl, and I hear him chuckling to himself behind me all the way down the stairs.

Lunch is in the dining room, a simple set-up of a large double-handled cast-iron pot with a dipping ladle, myriad mismatched bowls, and a sliced baguette on a breadboard along with curls of butter. It reminds me of being back in the children's home, where I lived before I was fostered out. But there it was a case of too many hungry mouths and never any second helpings.

The adults sit around the table while the kids are banished to the lounge, where there's a plastic tablecloth put on the floor for them. Hazel, Sarah, and Mirabelle volunteer to keep watch so there are no fights or spillages.

'We love them dearly, but it's nice to have some adult time too,' says Jennifer with a sigh of relief.

As well as her and Allan at the table, there are Simon and Kate, and … the black sheep, aka Kirk. Mid-thirties, dark-haired, lean, and intellectual, he's not as outgoing as the other McAdams siblings. He seems to prefer hanging around in the background or observing from over the top of his phone. Bailey gave me a brief rundown of his brother's relationship status on the drive back since I was curious (and wary about what his deal is). Apparently, he's a single dad who looks after 10-year-old Amy and 12-year-old Michael. Their mother, Liana, decided that she wanted to be a bigger fish in a bigger pond and took off to Hollywood to pursue an acting career. Kirk was lumped with childcare when the kids were 6 and 4. But according to Bailey, he never complained about it and is a good dad to them.

'What about Liana? Does she stay in touch?'

'Occasionally. Last we heard, she'd made some actor friends and was doing the audition rounds. Who knows, we might see her pop up in a movie one day.'

'Wow,' I say, not offering any opinion on the matter. To

be honest, my own experience with my biological mother isn't dissimilar. Maybe Kirk and I have more in common than I first thought. But the shrewd look in his eyes always puts me on guard. My spidey senses tell me to be careful around him. I'm proven right to be cautious when, before I've barely taken a sip of leek and potato soup, the Kirk interrogation begins.

'So how did you two meet?'

Bailey says blithely, 'We met at a Christmas party—'

I kick his foot under the table. 'In early December,' I add quickly.

'So you guys have been together only a few weeks then?'

'But it feels like forever.' Bailey puts his arm around my shoulder, and my body stiffens at his sudden nearness. 'As soon as she threw that Santa hat at me, it was all on.' He brushes my cheek lightly with his lips, and I smile tightly. Oh, OK, we're doing the kissing thing, are we?

Kate chortles. 'She threw a Santa hat at you?'

'I was being annoying.' I'm surprised to hear him admit this.

'That doesn't sound like you at all, Bails,' says Simon, grinning.

'He wasn't really,' I say. 'I was just a bit overwhelmed. He had a lot of festive wear happening ...' I gesture at Bailey's outfit. He's changed into yet another Christmas jumper. This one is designed to look like an elf uniform with red-and-white-striped sleeves, a black belt, and gold buttons. There's even a small embroidered candy cane poking out of the belt.

'I'm surprised you didn't run a mile,' says Kirk. 'Bailey is a walking Hallmark card this time of year.'

'Oh, I've gotten used to it.' Surprisingly, I have. His silly jumpers are ridiculous, but I like the way he doesn't care what anyone thinks.

'Hey!' Bailey protests. 'It's not my fault I'm a Christmas fanatic. Blame my mother.'

'It's true,' says Jennifer. 'I possibly overindulged on carols and Christmas cake when he was in the womb.'

Kirk's attention returns to me.

'You're staying for Bailey's birthday, I take it?'

'Uh ...' Shit, is it his birthday soon? He didn't say anything!

'You do know it's his birthday?' Kirk pounces on my hesitation.

'Yes, definitely,' I reply, looking him straight in the eye.

'Leave her alone, Kirk. It doesn't matter,' says Bailey sharply.

'So what date is it?' Kirk persists, ignoring Bailey. Everyone seems to be curiously awaiting my answer. I see Kate and Simon exchange a quizzical look.

I open my mouth to say 'We haven't discussed it ...' But Bailey taps my hand under the table. He presses two fingers, then four and then three into my palm. So his birthday is either the 9th or 27th. It can't be the 9th because it's already gone. It must be ... 'The 27th, of course,' I say confidently.

Kirk looks mollified, and Bailey gives my fingers a gentle squeeze. Phew, quick thinking on his part. I passed the test—for now. I have the feeling Kirk isn't going to let up until he catches us out. Even more annoying is that I was hoping to sneak away after Christmas Day. But now it seems I have to spend another three nights in Bailey's bed!

Chapter 14

The rest of the day passes in a blur of Christmas prep. I'm tasked with making chestnut, bacon, and cranberry stuffing for the chicken while Bailey works on his pudding. Various other family members come and go, depending on what they're bringing to the table, so to speak. At one point, I'm bumping elbows with Hazel as she chops broccoli and carrots. The next, I'm having a conversation with Simon about going vegan.

'I'm two months in, and it's been generally OK,' he says. 'I haven't missed meat at all. Christmas will be the true test.' He eyes the chicken, into which I'm currently ramming stuffing, and licks his lips. I get the feeling most of the nut roast he's making might end up in the bin.

Someone hooks up a Bluetooth speaker to their phone, and carols tinkle away in the background. Strangely, I don't mind. Snow is falling outside the window; and in this warm, convivial atmosphere, carols feel appropriate. It's nicer than having them blasted at you in the shops anyway.

'We try and do as much as possible on Christmas Eve so we can all relax tomorrow and enjoy it,' Jennifer tells me, glazing a ham on the other side of the table. 'No point in everyone being stuck in the kitchen all day.'

'Hear, hear! I'm all for that,' says Bailey. 'Holly, try this and let me know what you think.'

He dips his finger into a caramel-coloured sauce he's been whisking and proffers it to me.

'Er, I'll just use a spoon,' I say.

'Don't be silly. Just taste it.' He waves his finger in front of my nose, and to stop him from making a fuss, I suck the end of it. A hit of rich, sweet caramel with underlying flavours of rum and spice invades my mouth. It tastes so delicious I can't help sucking more of his finger to catch the drips.

Bailey watches me, amused. 'Good, huh?'

Red-faced, I return to my chicken. 'It's OK,' I mumble. 'Maybe a touch more rum.'

'On it,' he says. He bumps his hip gently against mine, and I shift away, confused.

Is he trying to flirt with me? Or is this part of the Holly and Bailey show? I'm the kind of person who doesn't respond well to ambiguity. It's too easy for wires to be crossed. I'd prefer to think he doesn't genuinely like me so I don't do anything to make a fool of myself. I make a mental note to stay off the alcohol—of any kind.

'Actually, I wouldn't add any more rum,' I tell him quickly. 'It's fine as it is.'

In the late afternoon, the festive spirit is taken up a notch with the McAdams family tradition of trimming the tree. A corner of the lounge is readied for a tall fir tree, which has apparently been stationed round the side of the house in a large black plastic pot. It still has snow on its branches and needs five people to lug it in.

'Dad has been nurturing this one for a few years now. We'll take it outside afterwards and plant it,' says Bailey, seeing me staring up at the tip of the eight-foot tree almost touching the ceiling.

'That's good. I hate how commercial Christmas trees are just dumped afterwards. I can see them brown and twisted, poking out of the bin from my flat window. It's depressing.'

'I know. But you don't have to worry about that here.' He opens a big box that contains baubles of different sizes and tinsel in various colours. 'Want to help me and the kids do the branches on this side?'

'OK.' I've never actually decorated a Christmas tree, so this is a first for me. It turns out to be more fun than I expected. Bailey and I kneel down to make sure the kids put the tinsel on evenly and don't crush the baubles in their chubby fists.

After a while, my knees get tired, and Charlie insists on sitting on my lap. So I sit cross-legged, and he settles in. We watch Bailey lift kids to attach bright baubles and tinsel higher up the tree. The room smells fresh and woodsy.

Hazel peers round from the other side to see where Charlie is. She smiles when she sees where he's sitting. 'Ah, he likes you. He's usually quite shy with new people.'

Charlie leans back against me and sucks his thumb contentedly. It seems being with Bailey is good enough for him to trust me. It feels alien, yet not entirely unpleasant. I'm not used to being around little kids or having them like me so wholeheartedly.

'Uncle Bailey, lift me up! I want to do the angel,' pleads Susie, capering around him when the tree decorations are nearly complete.

Bailey glances down at me. 'I was thinking Holly could do it since she hasn't before, and you did it last year.'

'Awww!' Susie pouts.

'It's OK. Let her do it. I don't mind,' I say, not sure what's involved. But Mirabelle takes Susie aside and talks to her about *sharing*, which I'm not sure Susie appreciates, judging from the grumpy look on her face. Sasha doesn't seem bothered. She's decorating herself with bits of stray blue and silver tinsel.

Hazel removes Charlie from my lap, and Bailey grabs my hand and pulls me up.

'What do I have to do?' I ask, feeling pressured.

'It's easy,' he says. 'You just sit on my shoulders and

place the angel up on top. We'll turn the tree lights on after dinner.'

'Where's the angel?'

'Here.'

Bailey carefully unwraps a tissue paper package and hands me a sizeable wooden doll with a finely painted face. The 'angel' is dressed in a delicate white skirt with a netting overlay embellished with silver sequins. She has a fluff of silver fur for her top and silver wings. Her blonde hair is in a topknot secured by a string of pearls.

'She lights up,' he explains. 'Under the skirt.'

I tip the doll over and see there's a battery case. I switch it on, and the skirt glows with tiny fairy lights.

'Oooh! Aaah!,' says everyone.

I get the feeling this is the critical moment of the whole proceedings, so I don't want to stuff it up. Unfortunately, I'm not that athletic nor good with heights.

'How are we going to do this?'

'Maybe stand on the arm of the couch, and I'll crouch in front of you so you can swing your legs over my shoulders.'

'Isn't there a ladder?'

'No, we don't need one. It's fine. Come on.'

I give the angel to Hazel as I need both hands to manoeuvre.

Somehow, I manage to clamber onto his shoulders, and

Hazel hands me the angel reverently. 'Don't drop her.'

'I'll try not to,' says Bailey from between my thighs.

'I think she meant the angel,' I mutter.

We proceed towards the tree when Bailey suddenly gets it into his head to swerve, bypassing the tree altogether. He does some silly dance, causing me to bounce around on his shoulders. He must be pulling funny faces as well as the kids are screeching with laughter.

'Uncle Bailey, stop! My tummy hurts.' Sasha is doubled over.

'What the hell are you doing?' I hiss, wanting to get it over with.

He's not listening, so I grab one of his ears and twist it. That gets his attention.

'Ow!'

'Tree. Now.'

'Yes, miss. Sorry, miss.' Now it seems he's rolling his eyes as the kids are giggling and copying him.

I tug his ear to steer him towards the tree.

'OK, OK, I'm going! Don't pull my ear off.'

The adults are all looking on, amused at our antics, apart from Kirk. Oops. I let go of Bailey's ear and pat his head.

'Sorry, sweetie.'

'That's more like it.' He approaches the tree, and I brush aside fir needles so they don't stab me in the eyes.

'Any time now would be good,' says Bailey with his face in the tree.

I place the angel on the topmost sticking-up branch, making sure her skirts are arranged nicely.

'Done!' I announce proudly.

Everyone whoops and claps.

Bailey backs out of the tree; and before I have time to wonder how I'm getting down, I'm propelled off his shoulders onto the couch, and he falls on top of me. More laughter erupts, making me want to yell, 'We're not a comedy act!'

I rub my thigh where Bailey's elbow has dug into it.

'Sorry, I tripped, accidentally on purpose,' he says in a muffled voice from the depths of my armpit.

'So I gathered,' I say dryly.

'Next year, Susie can do it. You're off the hook.'

It's only when we extricate ourselves and reassure everyone we're fine do I realise what he's said. Next year? Why will I be here next year? Unless ... Does Bailey actually see this going somewhere? Confusion makes me sway a little on my feet, and I knock into his arm.

'Whoa, you OK?'

'I think I might be concussed.'

He feels my forehead, and I close my eyes briefly as his cool hand gently soothes my brow. 'You are pretty hot,' he says in a low voice, tracing his thumb down the side of my cheek, and I shiver. From the way his brown eyes are intently gazing into mine, his meaning is pretty clear.

Heat rushes to my face. 'I think my brain is addled too,' I say breathlessly.

Bailey grins and gives my hand a squeeze. 'A McAdams family Christmas will do that to you.'

After a brief dinner of toasted sandwiches and leftover soup, we all gather in the lounge for the lighting of the tree. Bailey's gone off to his room for some reason, and when he walks back into the lounge, I can't help stifling a laugh. He's wearing a terrible jumper. It's the worst one yet—black with multiple strings of red and green Christmas lights and white fluffy piping to look like snow. There are matching squishy red and green baubles sewn on at intervals all over it. He comes over and sits down next to me on the couch.

'You really have no shame, do you?' I whisper, flicking one of his baubles.

He shrugs. 'Not really.'

I pull at it to see how firmly it's secured, and he holds my hand tightly so I can't pluck it off.

'Behave yourself. It's tree time.'

'Later then,' I mutter. 'Bauble showdown in your room.'

'It's a date,' he whispers in my ear, and a small thrill erupts in the pit of my stomach.

He's not acting anymore, surely? It doesn't feel fake—on my side anyway. The night is suddenly full of possibilities. Somehow, I don't think we'll be needing a cushion barrier if this is headed where I think it is.

The lounge plunges into darkness, causing everyone to go 'ooooh', and then the Christmas tree lights are switched on. It's a white twinkling explosion that hurts my retinas. There are so many lights swathed around the tree that it does a good job of lighting the whole room.

'Magical,' says Bailey.

'It is quite something,' I reply, staring up at my glowing angel in pride of place at the top.

Allan hands out steaming mugs of mulled wine for the adults (the kids get hot chocolate and marshmallows) along with squares of creamy fudge to nibble on.

I sip my wine and nestle my head against Bailey's baubled shoulder, feeling sleepy and content. Out of the corner of my eye, I see Kirk looking over to us and whispering to his son, Michael. What now? Bailey and I are behaving like a normal couple would, aren't we? I wish he would just leave us alone.

Shortly after, there's a movement behind the couch, and I look up to see a bunch of leaves with white berries hanging over my head. My stomach drops into my shoes. Shit. Mistletoe. I could kill Kirk. He's told Michael to do it to make it as awkward as possible for us.

Bailey looks up too, then at me uncertainly.

'Go on!' calls Allan. 'It's good luck!'

People are smiling at us. Lord, this is going to happen whether I like it or not. Maybe I can make it funny. I grab Bailey's cheeks with both hands and give him a noisy juicy smooch on the lips. Everyone laughs.

'Go, Holly! Girl power!' says Sarah, raising a fist in salute.

Bailey's cheeks are fiery red. I think he's more embarrassed than I am. Michael moves off and hangs the mistletoe over Simon and Kate, who oblige with a tasteful peck on the lips. Oh, that's probably what we should have done. Cringe.

Bailey is looking down and won't catch my eye. 'I think I might turn in. It's been a long day,' he murmurs, downing the rest of his wine.

'Oh, OK. I'll come too,' I say.

He shrugs. 'Stay if you like.'

'No, I don't mind,' I insist.

Why is he acting so weird? He didn't seem to mind holding hands and carrying on before. Did I take it too far? I mentally kick myself for thinking something more was going on when it's obviously not.

Crumpet seems happy enough cuddled up with Sarah, so

I plaster on a pleasant smile. We say goodnight, and I follow Bailey into the lit hallway. I'm dreading being alone with him now. How embarrassing.

'Are you OK?' I ask him.

He nods and gestures for me to go first up the stairs. Halfway up, I feel a tug on the back of my cardie. I look round into Bailey's face as he's almost level with me.

'Sorry for the abrupt exit.'

'Well, if you were tired ...'

'I wasn't tired. I ... just had to leave because of ...' He nods down at himself.

I frown, not understanding.

'When you kissed me, I got ... I didn't want anyone to see.'

God, I'm thick. 'Oh! They probably didn't. It was kind of dark.' I don't really know what else to say. 'Sorry I gave you an erection' doesn't seem appropriate.

We're standing so close I can see flecks of gold in his irises. His breath is sweet and spicy. Feeling the urge to kiss him properly, I lean forward and brush my lips against his, and he pulls me to him. Our lips meld together in a warm mulled-wine-infused kiss that gives me tingles all the way down my spine. It lasts only a moment, but it feels like time stands still.

Bailey gives a deep sigh. 'Finally.'

'Does that make your issue better or worse?' I ask, already knowing the answer.

'Worse. Much, much worse.'

Chapter 15

I yank Bailey's bauble jumper off over his head the minute we're in his moonlit room.

'Hey, careful! That's got at least another two Christmases in it.' But he doesn't complain when my hands go up under his T-shirt and run over his smooth muscular chest. With a growl, he backs me towards the bed; and we topple onto it, kissing frantically. He snakes a hand under my top and squeezes my breast while I devour his neck and collarbone. He tastes so good. I can't get enough of him. He unzips my jeans and pushes them, along with my knickers, down around my thighs.

I'm not sure if he means for that to happen, but I feel I should say something at this point to clarify things before they go too far. 'Uh, maybe we should talk about this,' I gasp as his hand moves down my stomach, heading south.

Bailey stops and looks at me. I can see his eyes glinting, one eyebrow raised. 'Really? Right now?'

I sit up, trying to calm my breathing. 'It's just ... Well, are you doing this because you have to? I don't want to force you into anything.'

He chuckles softly. 'I'm not that much of a pushover. I

wouldn't be doing this if I didn't want to.' He takes my hand and places it on his bulging crotch. I squeeze gently, and he groans. 'See, I'm not pretending.'

Maybe it will be OK. He wants me. I want him.

'Let's get into bed,' I say, making my mind up on the spot.

'Really? You're cool with this?' He gestures between us.

'Yes,' I say, unhooking my bra.

Bailey immediately bounces up off the bed and removes his jeans at breakneck speed. I can almost hear what he's thinking: 'Quick, before she changes her mind!'

Before I get into bed, I run swiftly over to the corkboard, turn the photo of him and Rosalie over, and put the thumbtack through her head.

'Why did you do that?' Bailey asks when I'm snuggled under the covers with him. He runs a warm hand over my back, and I shiver from his touch.

'Because I don't like to think of her hurting you.'

'Ah.' He shifts closer so our bodies are touching.

'Plus I don't want her looking at us.'

'Fair enough.'

Christmas morning

Soft kisses move up my thighs, and I shift my legs apart.

A tongue starts moving inquisitively, and soon, my eyes are practically rolling back in my head. I gasp as pleasure racks my core. 'Uhhh,' I groan, squeezing Bailey's head between my thighs like a vice.

When I've finished twitching, the man himself pops up from beneath the covers, hair mussed and cheeks dimpling in a grin. 'Merry Christmas,' he says, sliding up next to me; and I roll in for a hug and grasp his extremely nice butt, which I can't get enough of.

Downstairs, there are squeals interspersed with dull thuds.

'Your nieces and nephews are up,' I murmur dozily.

He nuzzles my cheek. 'Yeah, sounds like it.' He kisses me, our tongues entwine, and happiness infuses my body. Bailey is a great kisser, and he definitely likes to give more than he receives. I thought I would feel awkward or shy, but everything we've done feels so natural. It's like we know exactly what the other person needs. I stroke his arm, feeling more relaxed than I have in years.

He shakes his hair into place, props himself up on one elbow, and gives me a slow grin. I have to restrain myself from going gaga over his dimples. He is officially the cutest guy I've ever been with (not that there have been that many—we're talking single figures here).

'How are you this morning?' he asks.

I stretch out, rubbing my foot against his leg. 'Full of oxytocin.'

'That's romantic.'

'What can I say? I believe in the science behind social bonding.'

Bailey smirks. 'Is that what we've been doing? "Socially bonding"?'

'Well, yes. Physical interaction releases oxytocin. It's a well-known fact.'

'And here I was thinking we were getting it on because we liked each other.'

'Well, that may be a small part of it.'

'Only a small part?' He frowns. 'Holly, I—'

What he's about to say is interrupted by the door opening, and I yank the bedsheets up over my breasts.

Sarah's face appears in the crack with her hand over her eyes. 'I'm not looking, I promise! Crumpet wanted to come and say hi. He's been fed. I think he was missing you. Bye!' She opens the door wider, still with her hand over her eyes, and Crumpet pushes through and jumps up on the bed into my arms. 'Oh, and merry Christmas!'

'Merry Christmas!' Bailey calls after her.

'Do you think any more of your family are coming in?' I ask him, hugging Crumpet.

'Possibly. I'll get us some breakfast. Do you like eggs on

toast?'

'Uh, yes.'

'I'll bring them up. With a cup of tea?'

'Sounds fantastic.' I watch as Bailey rises from the bed, his naked body on full display. He doesn't seem to mind me perving at him as he hunts for his jeans, boxers, and T-shirt from last night. He picks up the bauble jumper, shoots me a look, and grins. 'Might just wear a hoodie.'

'Very wise,' I say.

He blows me a kiss from the doorway. 'Enjoy your lie-in. Back soon.'

Hmm, he's kind of fantastic too.

Despite the lack of sleep, I don't think I've ever been in this good a mood on Christmas Day. After handing me a tray with my eggs, Bailey says he's going to hit the shower. But his farewell kiss goes on longer than expected.

'I should eat these before they get cold,' I say, finally breaking our lip-lock.

'Good point. Otherwise, I'm going to end up back in bed with you.'

'Not a bad way to spend Christmas morning,' I reply jauntily, cutting into a poached egg lightly sprinkled with salt and pepper. Thick orange yolk oozes out. Mmm, organic, farm fresh—what a treat.

'Don't tempt me. I've got a lot to do today,' he says,

rummaging in his bag for, I assume, fresh clothes.

'I thought we did most of the food prep yesterday?' I ask.

'Trust me, there's an agenda.'

'Like what?'

'You'll see.' He sidles towards the door and slips out before I can see what he's holding in his arms. Odd. Crumpet jumps down and follows him, which is good. Otherwise, he'll look at me dolefully until I share my breakfast with him, and I want it all to myself.

I've just finished gobbling down the most delicious eggs on buttery toast I think I've ever eaten, along with an amazing cup of tea, and am lying back on the pillows, replete, when Bailey returns. I take one look at him and let out a whoop of laughter. 'You've got to be kidding me!'

He's in full elf regalia for the occasion. That consists of his elf jumper from yesterday. But he's also added a pair of green trousers, long pointy green shoes that curl up, a felt hat, plus the elf ears from the party.

He purses his lips and looks mock offended. Then he tries to saunter nonchalantly into the room with the bells on the end of his shoes and hat jingling. It makes me laugh even harder.

'You look ridiculous,' I tell him, wiping my eyes on the sheet.

'I know, but the kids love it.'

He's right. As soon as we enter the lounge, where everyone's gathered, the kids leap up excitedly and start yelling 'Present time! Present time!' It seems Uncle Bailey is the official present hander outer. I half expect to see the rest of his family dressed up too, but no, it's just Bailey. It seems weird to think I've been rolling around in bed all night—with an elf. I shake my head to get rid of the ensuing images.

There are a pile of presents that have 'magically' appeared under the Christmas tree, and the little stockings dangling from the mantelpiece are full. A fire is crackling in the grate, and snow is falling outside the window. I feel like I'm in one of those feel-good Christmas movies. Like the over-the-top desserts on the first night, it's all a bit overwhelming.

On the way to the lounge, Bailey reassured me it wouldn't take long as they have a 'one present' rule. But that, it appears, is for the adults. The kids are fair game, and they rip into their stockings and then the presents under the tree from 'Santa'. Soon, there's paper and toys scattered all over the carpet. I'm awkwardly sitting off to the side on a footstool, watching on and not really feeling involved. This isn't my family or my reality. I'm in the way.

When the adults have all had their presents and exclaimed, 'It's just what I wanted', et cetera, I breathe a sigh of relief. Thank God that's over with.

Until Kirk pipes up, 'What about Holly? Doesn't she get a present from Santa?'

Dammit, it's going to look suspicious if Bailey doesn't give me something. Why can't Kirk just keep his mouth shut?

'Ah, yes, Holly,' says Bailey in the squeaky elf voice he's been putting on. 'I have something for her.' He does a leaping jig over to the Christmas tree, making his bells ring and the kids giggle. I shrink down, thinking that he's going to make a big show of there not being a present because I've been a naughty girl or something. But he pulls out a Santa stocking that's nestled at the back of the tree. Oh no, what's he doing?

There's another jingling jig back over to me, and he hands me the Santa stocking, which I can feel has several items inside it. 'Merry Christmas!' he squeaks, and I stare at him questioningly.

'What's this?' I mouth.

He grins and mouths back, 'Just open it.'

Hesitantly, I pull apart the Velcro fastening and look inside. Susie and Sasha are peering over my shoulders, dying to see what it is. I start drawing out a bunch of miscellaneous Christmas paraphernalia: a small *Frozen* make-up kit, elf ears, a silver tiara, gold bracelets, a glass gemstone-encrusted necklace, and a wand with a glitter star on the end that lights up when I wave it. I stare at the items blankly.

'Susie and Sasha, do you want to help Holly become my elf girlfriend?' asks Bailey, and they nod excitedly.

I'm about to protest, but Bailey whispers, 'Just go with it.' So I have no choice but to sit as still as a statue with my eyes closed as the girls carefully put eyeshadow on my lids, then dab on lipstick and blusher and slide the bracelets up my arms. Bailey fastens the necklace and puts on my elf ears.

'There!' exclaims Susie, settling the tiara on my head. 'She's an elf princess! So pretty!'

Bailey beams, handing me the wand. 'She is indeed.' Before I can stop him, he whips out his phone and puts his cheek next to mine.

I can't help smiling at the selfie he takes. We do look pretty cute as elves, though our expressions are different: me mock frowning and him with his infectious grin.

His thoughtfulness at including me in everything makes sudden tears prick behind my eyes. I squeeze his hand. 'You didn't have to do this, but thank you.'

'Well, I hope you don't mind. But I knew you'd make a beautiful elf, and I was right,' he says, slinging an arm around my shoulder.

What's left of the ice around my heart slowly slides off and falls with a plop onto the floor. I'm still not exactly sure how, but Bailey has single-handedly managed to pierce through my brittle demeanour and soften me up. I feel like a more malleable marzipan version of myself. A little mulled wine, a night of passion, and now I'm wearing elf ears. For Holly Driver, self-confessed loner and hater of all things Christmas, this is unthinkable behaviour. I'm not sure who this new girl is, but I'm starting to quite enjoy myself.

Chapter 16

Bailey's kindness, boyish charm, and mischievous nature are an irresistible combination. Every time his hand accidently on purpose brushes mine it sparks a deep yearning that I try to fight but find myself succumbing to. I can't seem to think about anything else but spending the rest of the afternoon in bed with him. But lunch is the main Christmas meal, and we're both in the kitchen helping prepare it, so disappearing upstairs isn't an option.

But I can't resist a comment to him under my breath when his mum and Hazel are chatting over at the sink. 'Any chance of a sneaky elvish rendezvous after lunch?' I say it lightly and hope, since we're still in costume, it sounds cute rather than needy.

The corner of his mouth quirks, and he presses his warm arm against mine. The electricity sparking between us gives me goosebumps.

Bailey clears his throat and says loudly, 'I'll just go and grab some potatoes from the cellar.'

Hazel looks round. 'Yes, we'll need to get them in the oven pronto. Do you want a hand?'

'It's OK. Holly can help me,' he replies quickly.

'Can you guys bring up a few more bottles of wine too?'

'Sure.'

Bailey grabs a wicker basket, and I follow him to a door at the far side of the kitchen. He opens it and tugs on a dangling piece of string. Down below, a bare light bulb glows yellow. 'After you,' he says.

I peer into the depths, and a waft of cold earth-scented air invades my nostrils. 'I don't know. It looks a bit spooky.'

'Well, it's the best I can do at short notice. Unless you can wait three hours? Lunch is usually finished by two, but then there's the clean-up ...'

Aha! He's been so touchy-feely with me during lunch prep. I *knew* he was thinking along the same lines.

'So the potatoes are down here?' I say brightly and take off down the rickety wooden steps. Bailey closes the door behind us with an evil cackle, as if to insinuate I'm caught in his wicked trap. But even if he's offering a few kisses in a potato cellar, I'll take them.

The cellar is a square brick-walled and stone-floored space with a strip of narrow window at the top on one side, covered over with snow. There's not much down here except some dusty wine bottles in a rack, a bench with some tools, and a few crates of potatoes lined up by the walls. Surprisingly, there's also a cracked leather couch and a bookcase with faded dog-eared covers. I pull one out at random and look at it. '*Catch-22.* Is this a man cave?'

'Dad used to escape down here when there was too much noise and chaos upstairs.'

'It's freezing.' I pull down my cardigan sleeves over my hands and rub my arms. 'I hope he brought a hot-water bottle or a blanket.'

Bailey dumps the baskets near a crate of potatoes. 'Aye. It's balmier in summer,' he says, not looking at me.

I stand there, feeling awkward. Now we're down here, I'm not sure if I've gotten the wrong end of the stick. Maybe he really did want help with the potatoes and not to snog me after all?

'Bailey ...' I say helplessly, not knowing how to communicate that I want him badly.

Perhaps my voice conveys some of what I'm feeling because he scoops an arm around me, pulls me close, and covers my lips with his. The relief of kissing him again is palpable. My body relaxes. It's like coming home. I thread my fingers through his hair, accidentally dislodging one of his latex elf ears, which falls on the floor.

'Oops, sorry.'

He laughs. 'Maybe we should do this without ears.'

'Without clothes would be even better,' I say boldly.

'Hmm, we've got exactly ten minutes before someone

opens the door to find out what's happened to us.'

'There's no privacy in this house,' I grumble.

'Welcome to my world.' Bailey looks at his watch. 'We can discuss this further, but I'd rather kiss you if that's all right.'

'Well, since we're here ...' I give in to the lure of his lips. The sight of two human-sized elves making out must look pretty funny, but I don't care. At this point, Bailey could be dressed as a giant candy cane, and I'd still be into him.

We're just getting warmed up on the couch when the door at the top of the stairs opens, and Hazel calls down, 'What are you elves doing down there? Snogging? We need the potatoes asap!'

Bailey snickers into my hair. 'Told you.'

Christmas afternoon

Christmas lunch is delicious, including the famous flambé pudding, but I can't seem to eat much. All I can think about is how good Bailey's tongue felt in my mouth, the weight of his warm body moving against mine, and how many minutes I have to wait until we can finish what we started.

When we're left alone for a few precious minutes, washing up at the sink, he teases me with promises of going upstairs for a 'nap', then changes his mind, saying we could stay down here and 'play board games' instead. He's working me up into a frenzy of want, and he knows it. When the last dish is dried, I grab his hand and dig my nails into his palm. 'Let's go. Now.'

Bailey bites his lip and gives me a scorching look that makes my thighs tremble. 'I just need to talk to Kirk.'

'What about?'

'Pretty sure he has condoms. You know ... just in case,' he adds.

'Oh.'

Bloody hell. We didn't technically have sex last night, but things are moving in that direction. So much for being horrified about sleeping together in his family home. I've certainly changed my tune. But it doesn't feel wrong. It feels very right.

But still ... 'Why does it have to be Kirk?'

Bailey shrugs. 'Because I know he's been online dating.'

Doesn't mean he's scored, I think snidely.

'OK, where is he?'

'In the lounge, I think.'

We walk in, holding hands, to discover an audience of kids watching a Christmas movie. At least I think it's a movie, but then I register what it really is, and the blood drains from my face. Kirk's hooked up his computer to the massive wall TV and is playing TikTok videos. I watch in horror as a young guy dressed as Santa drunkenly rides a bike through a village and falls into a duck pond. It's got 5,000 likes and 300 comments. *Way less than mine.*

The kids fall about, laughing hysterically.

'Play it again, Uncle Kirk!' gasps Susie.

Bailey beckons to Kirk to come over to us, and he holds up a finger. 'Just a second. This looks like a good one.'

Oh god. 'Please tell him to stop playing them!' I hiss to Bailey.

He looks at me enquiringly, hearing the urgency in my tone. 'How come?'

'TikTok isn't for kids!'

Simon hears me from where he's playing Monopoly with Kate, Hazel, and Allan. 'Are these videos suitable, Kirk?'

'It's fine. TikTok doesn't allow X-rated stuff.'

Jennifer looks up from the book she's reading. 'It seems harmless.' She peers at me over her reading glasses. 'Are you OK, Holly? You look like you've seen a ghost.'

I nod my head slowly, unable to tear my eyes from the screen. Maybe it won't appear. What are the chances?

The kids are now laughing at a bunch of golden Labradors being taken for a walk on triple speed. They're dressed as reindeers with brown felt antlers and accompanied by the clown song.

Bailey is chuckling as well. 'I'm not on TikTok, but

maybe I should be. These vids are funny.'

Seeing he has a captivated audience, Kirk says, 'They're US ones. I'll type in "Christmas UK" and see what comes up.'

My lungs tighten, and I find it hard to breathe. Oh nooooo! The chances just got a hell of a lot better.

Kirk starts scrolling through the top videos, then widens his eyes and looks straight at me. On the TV screen, my face has appeared in one of the thumbnails, but no one else has seen it yet. The back of my neck breaks out in a sweat.

'Here's an interesting one,' he says in a sing-song tone. *Don't you dare, you fuck!*

But I've obviously done something to Kirk in a former life. He clicks on it and *turns up the volume!*

My face fills the entire fifty-inch screen. You can even see a small red zit on my nose.

'Yeah, so listen up, TikTokers ...' My voice blares into the room like a loudspeaker. Everyone gasps in unison, and all heads turn as one to me. I stare at the wall, not brave enough to look at Bailey. It's bad enough that he dropped my hand as soon as he heard what I was saying. I sound like a drunken lunatic.

'Kirk, *turn it off!*' I cry, knowing the next bit is worse. But he either doesn't hear me or refuses to comply.

It's too late. There I am in the shower cap, swaying and

slurring and holding the stupid hairdryer. Saying Santa is an arsehole and his elves are worse. Going on about how I hate reindeers, carols, and eggnog. Then giving the fingers and wishing everyone a crappy Christmas. You could hear a pin drop. The entire lounge is riveted.

I feel sick to my stomach. With 4.2 million views, 170,000 likes and 5,000 comments, my grinch rant is one of the top TikToks in the UK. And the most Christmassy family I've ever met has just seen it—on Christmas Day, no less!

When the 'Jingle Bells' music comes on and Lewis's face appears with his finger held to his lips, there are a few nervous titters. People don't know if they should laugh or not. But the kids aren't buying it.

'Why is Aunty Holly on the ClipClop video?' asks Susie suspiciously, peering at me over the back of the couch.

'Yeah, and why was she being so *mean?*' Sasha wants to know. She looks at me fearfully with a quivering lip and promptly bursts into tears, setting off Susie and then Charlie, who starts wailing at the top of his lungs. Hazel and Sarah rush over to comfort them.

'Maybe it's meant to be ironic? Isn't that right, Holly?' says Jennifer, giving me a half-hearted smile. She's trying to be comforting and positive, and I applaud her for it, but there's no saving me. I've scared the kids, and there's a definite feeling of animosity in the room. Everyone is frowning at me like I've shitted on their festive parade.

'What I want to know,' says Kirk clearly over the commotion, 'is why Lewis and Holly were drunk in his hotel room. Where exactly were you, Bails?'

I risk a look at Bailey, who's been quiet this whole time. His expression is stony, and my heart breaks for him. What I've done looks so dodgy, especially since Lewis is his friend and his previous girlfriend cheated on him. I should've said something so he didn't have to find out like this—in front of his whole family. Maybe we could've laughed it off together, shown a united front like we have up until now. By the look on his face, something tells me I'm on my own for this one.

Bailey doesn't reply to Kirk's question. Instead, he walks out of the room in silence and slams the door. Shit.

I hurry after him in a panic and catch up with him in the hallway. 'Bailey, wait! It's not what you think. Yes, Lewis and I were drunk. But nothing happened.'

Bailey stares at me coldly. 'You're in a viral TikTok posted by my friend. Did you not think to tell me about this?'

'I didn't want to involve you *because* Lewis is your friend,' I say miserably. 'I didn't ask him to post it. I've been trying to get it taken down! And he's gone AWOL. His phone keeps switching to voicemail.'

'That'd be because he's off-grid in the Faroe Islands.' He rubs his hand over his face. 'It's all making a lot more sense now why you were in Kingussie train station and why you booked into that awful guest house. You were running away.'

'Yes, I panicked! But I'm the innocent party in this!' I exclaim. 'Do you think I want my face plastered all over TikTok? It's been excruciating ... And bloody Lewis, he's just on holiday, having a fucking wonderful time!'

Bailey takes a deep breath. 'Lewis didn't force you to say those things. In fact, it looked to me like you were enjoying yourself,' he says tightly, and I shrink inside. Was I? I have no recollection of it at all, so I can't refute it. 'I think you should go upstairs. Take some time out.'

I'm about to say 'Stop treating me like a child', but by the clench of his jaw, I know this isn't the time to argue.

'Are you coming up too?'

'No, I need to do some damage control down here.'

I swallow. The sound of kids' wailing can still be heard from the lounge. Maybe it's best if I make myself scarce.

Chapter 17

I knew this was too good to be true. After all, this is real life, not some cheesy Christmas romcom movie, where the guy and the girl live happily ever after. Real life is when you get dealt the worst hand, and somehow, you have to make the best of it—relying only on yourself.

'It's better this way, buddy,' I say to Crumpet, who was rudely woken from his snooze on the bed by me bursting in. 'It was all getting way too intimate.' Crumpet drums his tail on the quilt in agreement. Falling for Bailey is tantamount to leaving myself open to the worst possible pain, and I don't know if I can take that risk with him. OK, I admit I'm not feeling the greatest right now. But my heart isn't ripped open, merely a bit bruised. I'll get over it.

Crumpet nuzzles my hand, and I feel guilty that I've been neglecting him. Here I am snogging Bailey in the potato cellar when I should've been spending time with my dog. What was I thinking? He whines a little, sensing my distress. As an emotional support pet, he truly is a godsend. No matter how bad things get, I can rely on Crumpet to be there for me. 'I'm sorry, I'm so sorry,' I babble, hugging him to me.

The afternoon drags on. I half expect Bailey to come up, but he doesn't, and I daren't go downstairs until I've spoken to him. Being in exile isn't much fun. There's nothing to do except feel sorry for myself or look at my phone, which has no 'merry Christmas' messages from the family or anyone else. I'm tempted to call Andrea for a heart-to-heart since she knows about the TikTok, but I don't want to disturb her on Christmas Day. So I send her a text instead: *Merry Christmas, hope you're having a nice day with your family!* She doesn't reply.

I remove my elf get-up and place the items carefully on the dresser. I still don't know why Bailey had all that with him. Were they meant to be for Susie and Sasha? Now I feel doubly bad I made them cry.

'I wish I'd never gone to Lewis's fucking party,' I say out loud. But then if I hadn't gone to the party, I never would've met Bailey. And if I hadn't been escaping from the TikTok, I wouldn't have been in Kingussie and bumped into him again. Each of my actions and reactions are tangled up in him.

A montage of images floods my brain: Bailey twisting round in the passenger seat to grin at me. Me whacking the bejesus out of him with a cushion. Him falling through the window of the guest house and saving me from a cold lonely night. Playing 'hand math' with me under the table to outsmart Kirk. Strutting into the lounge wearing his terrible bauble jumper. Our spine-tingling kiss on the stairs. Our night of passion under the duvet. Getting it on with him in the potato cellar ... Oh god. The longer I spend up here alone with my thoughts, the more it becomes clear: Bailey's the best thing that's ever happened to me, and I've fucked it up. Then my own tears arrive, falling down my cheeks and plopping onto Crumpet's back. What am I going to do?

Around six, someone knocks on the door. Outside there's a tray with a roast chicken & salad sandwich and a tall glass of chocolate milk, along with a bowl of dog food for Crumpet. Who did that? Bailey or one of his sisters? Starving, I wolf down the sandwich, and Crumpet digs in to his food too. I note there's no dessert for the naughty girl. I'll have to be content with my chocolate milk. But then I remember I still have the tinfoil-wrapped star cookies in the pocket of my bag. Hah!

I polish off the gingerbread cookies (mmm, tasty), wash them down with the chocolate milk, and that's my dinner. Prison rations. Everyone's downstairs tucking into leftovers and trying not to mention my name, I assume.

When it reaches nine, I give up waiting for Bailey, turn out the lights, and get into bed. If he ever does grace me with his presence, I'm going to apologise and hope that we can discuss what happened like rational adults. If that doesn't work, then I'm going to ask him to drive me to the train station tomorrow morning, and I'll pay him for the petrol. That's the big plan I've come up with. If he doesn't want anything more to do with me, at least I can leave with what dignity I have left intact.

When the door cracks open what seems like hours later and Bailey creeps in, I'm still awake, but with my eyes shut. He doesn't say anything to me, just removes his clothes and gets in. We lie there like two cardboard cut-outs, not speaking. He can probably tell I'm awake by my breathing. Now or never.

'I'm really sorry about what happened,' I say formally. 'If there's any way I can make it up to you and your family, please let me know. Everyone's been so kind to me, especially you.'

Bailey doesn't reply, and for a moment, I think he's going to leave me hanging. But then I sense him relax and shift towards me.

'Apology accepted,' he says.

I can't believe it's going to be that easy.

After a pause, he says 'So you're kind of a celebrity,' in a light, playful tone. He doesn't seem mad like he was before. I wonder what's been said downstairs.

'I guess,' I say just as lightly. 'If you believe in social

media fame, which I don't. Believe me, I've been doing everything I can to get it deleted.'

'Lewis is a prick for doing that without your consent,' he says, which surprises me. Is he on my side?

'I'm not taking sides,' he confirms quickly. 'What you said was pretty scathing. I know you're not a big fan of Christmas, but it was uncalled for.'

'I know. If I could take it back, I would.'

'I believe you.'

I let out a sigh, roll towards him, and bury my head in his shoulder. 'Thank you. That means a lot. What about your family? Do they hate me?'

'They don't hate you. They're just confused as to why you would say all that stuff. Mum gets it more since you said you were fostered out. She's an ex-social worker, so she's seen some things.'

'I guess I've always felt bitter because I never had a proper Christmas myself. I put on an act and say I hate Christmas, but deep down, I'm jealous of everyone who has that and takes it for granted. It must've all just come out when I was drunk and Lewis encouraged me to get it out of my system.'

Bailey's hand finds my arm and rubs it gently. I know it's meant to be comforting, but since he's wearing only boxers, it's difficult to concentrate.

'How do you feel now?' he asks.

Rather horny actually. No! Focus, Holly. You should be grateful he's even talking to you.

'I feel ... different. Being here with you and your family ... I've seen what a real Christmas looks like, and I liked being part of it.' I shift closer to his warm body, and he puts an arm around me and strokes my back. The relief I feel is palpable. Thank God he doesn't hate me.

'I know you haven't had it easy, but not everyone's out to get you. *I'm* not out to get you. You can trust me.' He yawns and adds sleepily, 'Anyway, we can hear what Lewis has to say for himself tomorrow.'

I suck in my breath. 'What?'

'Um, yeah. He always visits on Boxing Day and stays for my birthday. We usually try to visit a couple of distilleries. But this year, with the snow, it may not happen ...' He leaves the sentence hanging as I sit bolt upright.

'Speaking of telling each other things, don't you think you should've told me *that*?'

'Uh, I kind of forgot with everything else going on.' *Or he didn't think I'd still be around by then ...* 'He's bringing Moira, his girlfriend, too.'

'Bailey!' Grrr, I could murder him.

'Don't panic. It's a good thing! Now you can have it out with him and get him to delete the TikTok—if that's what you want.'

'Of course I want that. But ... I'm not good at confrontation.'

'You'll be fine. I'll support you. I'm as keen as you are to get it sorted out. Don't really want my elf girlfriend telling everyone she hates Santa's guts.' Bailey yawns again. 'Hey, do you mind if we go to sleep now? It's been a bit of a crazy day, and we didn't get much shut-eye last night.'

'Of course.'

'G'night then.' He kisses me on the temple and rolls over. 'Night.'

But as his breathing evens out, I lie awake wide-eyed and wired, digesting this shiny new nugget of information. Lewis *and* his girlfriend are coming here! I'm grateful that everything seems OK with Bailey and his family. But now there's a new challenge: confronting Lewis.

This is it. This is my chance to redeem myself. Or will I run away like a lily-livered lion as usual?

Chapter 18

Boxing Day

'Holly, do you want to go for a walk with me and Mirabelle and check on the sheep?' asks Sarah.

'Oh ... OK,' I reply, instantly on guard.

After the chat with Bailey last night, I've been released from exile and felt safe enough to come down to the kitchen with him for breakfast. My reception from his family when I walked into the room was a little on the awkward side, but it wasn't as bad as it could have been. There was no mention of yesterday's drama at all. Whatever Jennifer has been saying about foster children has gone some way towards helping my case. I just wish I knew exactly what it is she's been saying. Hopefully, nothing like 'Now, troops, Holly has obviously had a rough time of it. And her attitude towards Christmas is completely understandable. This is the time when she needs our patience and compassion the most. Please treat her kindly'.

I really don't want them pitying me.

So when I've just finished my last mouthful of toast and Sarah asks me to go for a walk, it's surprising, but not unexpected. She's showing that she's stepping up to the mark and doing her bit.

'Good idea,' chimes Bailey. 'I'll stay here since Lewis and Moira are meant to be arriving this morning.'

Excellent. That will be something to look forward to (not!).

Kirk, on the other side of the table, hoots. 'Is Lewis still coming?'

'As far as I know,' says Bailey. 'I haven't heard otherwise.'

'I can't wait to see how this plays out,' says Kirk, smirking at me. I smile back thinly. *Starved for entertainment, are we?* I still haven't forgiven him for playing the TikTok for the kids. I don't think I ever will. They're staying well clear of me, and I don't blame them. Aunty Holly has shown her true colours.

Fifteen minutes later, I'm crunching through the snow, wearing a borrowed coat and borrowed wellingtons. Crumpet comes too for some fresh air, and the air *is* decidedly fresh. After being stuck inside all day yesterday, the frozen fields at the back of the house stretching out yonder are a feast for the eyes.

'Pretty, isn't it?' comments Sarah as we wait for Mirabelle to climb a fence stile.

'It is,' I agree. 'Is this land all yours?'

She nods. 'It's a waste, really, since no one in my family is farming inclined. We could've been growing all sorts of things. Mum has a small veggie and herb patch near the house, but that's it.'

'Whose are the sheep then?'

'A neighbour's. He rents out the field for them to graze, but he's gone off on holiday. He rang to ask if we could keep an eye on them. There's a dry shed they can use at night. But they've been sheltering in there during the day as well since the snow is so heavy this year.'

'Ah.'

We crunch along in companionable silence, making our way towards a slate-roofed stone shed in the distance.

'So Mum mentioned that you were a foster kid?' Sarah says.

I nod.

'It's an option we considered. But then Hazel suggested we use a sperm donor and Mirabelle got pregnant with the girls. Now I'm thinking we should've looked into it more.'

'Fostering isn't for everyone,' I say. 'Sometimes people think they're being saintly by taking on a child that isn't theirs. But they never stop to think the child could be better off not being with them.'

'Are your foster family real stinkers?' she says bluntly.

OK, she's not skirting around anything. I'm a bit taken aback. How do I answer that?

'They're not the most convivial of people,' I reply carefully. 'And my sister, Violet, their real daughter, tends to make everything about her. I think she would've been better off as an only child.'

A memory surfaces of 8-year-old Violet snatching a second-hand Barbie doll that had been given to me at the children's home, whirling it over her head by the hair and throwing it out the window onto the road. Definitely not convivial.

'We'll be your sisters,' says Mirabelle, linking her arm in mine.

'Oh, you don't have to—'

'No, we *want* to. You're great. Much better for Bailey than that bitch Rosalie.' Mirabelle claps a hand over her mouth. 'I should not have said that.'

My interest is piqued. 'What was she like? He's told me a little, but not much.'

'Selfish,' says Sarah, linking my other arm. 'She made Bailey run around after her like she was Lady Muck. There was just something off about her. Then she cheated on him with his friend. He was seriously fucked in the head for ages after that. I think he had visions of settling down with her, but she had other ideas.'

I grimace. 'Poor Bailey. He didn't deserve that.'

'No, and if you hurt him, we'll track you down and make you pay.' Sarah punches her mittened fist lightly into my shoulder. 'I'm just joking,' she says with a laugh. 'Rosalie is still alive and well. But we didn't like seeing Bailey hurt.'

I don't doubt it. He's a beloved younger brother.

'I can tell he likes you, though.'

I glow a little at that. 'Really?'

'Yes, he's sensitive to the needs of others and injured animals too. He looked after an owl with a broken wing in a box when he was little.'

'Oh.'

'Its wing didn't mend properly, and it hopped around after him. We called him Harry Potter for months.'

I know she's intending to show Bailey in a good light as a caring guy, but to me, it sounds like I'm a fixer-upper project for him—someone he can look after and repair. But what if I'm irreparably broken? Bailey deserves someone who comes from a loving family, not a household of freaks.

After checking on the sheep, we go back via the road as it's clear of snow, though there are several puddles thick with ice, which Mirabelle makes us jump on to hear them crack.

'Such a satisfying crunch, don't you think?'

Back at the house, I'm feeling like I'm part of the family again and even playing a rather violent game of Snap with Bailey when he looks out the window as a silver BMW pulls up outside. He glances at me, and my gut twists. Showtime. Lewis is here.

Kirk has already opened the door and is greeting him, keen to get him inside for the next round of 'humiliate Holly', no doubt. I stand behind Bailey, hands sweating. Lewis comes in grinning with a holdall. He's wearing designer jeans, a white shirt, and a pinstriped blazer. His hair is slicked back, and he looks every inch the hotel mogul. Seeing him again brings his betrayal into sharp focus. How dare he do this to me? What an absolute jackass. He hasn't even bothered to message or ring me back.

Lewis steps forward to greet Bailey, then catches sight of me. The utter shock that passes across his face is quite satisfying. It's like he's seen the pope in Speedos at a Wet 'n' Wild. He stares at me, dumbfounded. 'Wha ...?'

'Lewis, you know Holly,' says Bailey smoothly.

'Of course I know Holly.' He opens his mouth and shuts it again. Whatever he wants to say is obviously not appropriate for the situation—namely 'What the fuck is she doing here?'

Our ambush of him is giving me more confidence. 'Hi,

Lewis,' I say, giving a small wave. He's followed by a pretty whippet-thin woman with razor-sharp cheekbones and shoulder-length highlighted Rachel-from-*Friends* hair.

'I'm Moira,' she says, holding out a bony hand to me.

'Pleased to meet you. I'm Holly, Bailey's girlfriend,' I reply, feeling supremely grateful when he casually drapes an arm around my shoulder to confirm it. But then I realise it's probably more of a possessive gesture to mark his territory. Either way, it's a good move as it boosts my confidence further.

Lewis's mouth hangs ajar at this revelation. I'm quite enjoying this. The rest of the McAdams family comes piling out to see who's here. Kids peek out from behind their parents' legs. Jennifer gives Lewis and then Moira a warm hug. 'Welcome! You made it through OK.'

'Yes, no problems. The roads were open ...' Lewis is still eyeing me as if I'm an apparition, trying to work out why I'm there.

Underneath the commotion, a female voice sounds from the doorway. 'Hello?'

The collective gaze falls upon a familiar-looking young woman standing on the threshold, grasping an overnight bag. Her eyes seek someone in the crowd, and she smiles when her gaze rests on Bailey. Now it's my turn to feel shock. It's Andrea from HR.

Chapter 19

'Come in, come in!' Jennifer, the hostess with the mostest, approaches Andrea, holding out her hand. 'Are you one of Bailey's friends too?'

'Yes, I'm Andrea,' she says with a laugh, shaking Jennifer's hand. She looks elegant in black-and-white-checked trousers and a powder-blue cashmere jumper, which offsets her pink cheeks. 'I hitched a lift with Lewis and Moira rather than drive,' she adds. 'My car conked out after dropping my parents off at the station, and I wanted to make sure I got here in time for the birthday celebrations. I hope it's OK.' She looks over to Bailey again, and yikes, this is flipping awkward. Any second now ... Andrea's eyes shift from him and flick over my face. Her smile falters. I can see her mind working overtime: *Holly's here? What's going on? Why is his arm around her? What the hell have I just walked into?*

She takes a step backwards, as if poised to run. But she's trapped, reliant on Lewis for transport. At that moment, I genuinely feel sorry for her, but not too sorry as she's obviously got designs on Bailey. What went on with them at the Christmas party? It must've been something for her to come all the way up here on Boxing Day with Lewis and Moira.

Bailey is silent. His fingers tighten on my shoulder imperceptibly. Kirk is looking at us quizzically as he tries to work out Andrea's involvement in our relationship. Good luck with that—I'm having difficulty myself.

'Bailey didn't mention you were coming, but of course, you're very welcome,' says Jennifer. 'It's a tight fit, but we'll find room. More the merrier, I always say!'

Bailey suddenly finds his voice and his manners, realising his silence is making things worse.

'Andrea! So great to see you. Thanks for coming up.' He goes over to relieve her of her bag and give her a kiss on the cheek. My stomach clenches.

'Right,' says Allan decisively. 'Lewis and Moira are in the annexe. Follow me.'

They head off outside, and Jennifer looks at Andrea with her head tilted to one side, considering. 'Come with me. I've got the perfect spot for you.' She grabs Andrea's bag off Bailey and hustles her upstairs with a small shake of her head at him. Hopefully she doesn't make up a bed for her in his room! Everyone else wanders back into the lounge now that the excitement is over ... and I can breathe again.

I prod Bailey's side. 'You never mentioned an annexe,' I mutter.

'Why do you think? I wanted you in with me.'

'Ah, sneaky. You also didn't mention ...' I jerk my chin in the direction of the stairs.

He plants a swift kiss on the top of my head. 'Sorry about that.'

'What is she doing here?'

'Ah, I vaguely remember discussing Boxing Day plans with Lewis at the party, and I must have invited her too. I'd had a few drinks. I can't really remember.'

'You're a shocker. She's taken it as a come-on.'

He wrinkles his nose. 'I don't think so. We just danced a bit. I was being an idiot as usual.'

'Really? Nothing else?'

'No! Just chatting and silly dancing.'

Hmm, I'm not sure Bailey's memory is 100 per cent reliable about that night. But how can I judge him when I was off my head?

In the kitchen, Bailey puts on the kettle to make tea and slides a plate of freshly made scones onto the table, along with a pot of strawberry jam, butter, and a small bowl of whipped cream.

'Did you make these?'

'Er, yes?'

'Wow, you're the first guy I've ever met who bakes scones,' I say in wonder. It's another really attractive feature about him. I'm half inclined to forgive him about the Andrea debacle. I do like a good scone.

'Stick with me, baby. I'm full of surprises,' he says, grasping me round the waist.

We're enjoying an alone-time kiss when Lewis barges into the room, catching us mid-clinch. He freezes. 'What the hell is going on?' He points a finger at me. 'The last time I saw you was tucked up in bed in my hotel room with a shower cap on. Now you're snogging my friend in front of a cream tea.' He rubs his forehead melodramatically. 'Am I going nuts?'

Moira comes into the room at that moment. 'Did someone say "cream tea"? Ooh yum, a Bailey special.' She sits down at the table and looks at me expectantly. 'White with no sugar, thanks.'

Huh, apparently, I'm making the teas. I head over to the cupboard to search for some mugs. I'm fully committed to confronting Lewis in a calm, civilised manner when the time is right. So I'm surprised to hear Bailey saying from behind me, 'Holly's here because of what you did.' Oh no, he's stealing my thunder!

'What *I* did?' Lewis sounds bewildered.

'On TikTok.'

'Huh?'

'Haven't you checked your account?'

'No, I've been on a social media hiatus.'

'Well, check it now.'

Bemused, Lewis pulls out his phone out of the back pocket of his jeans. I hold my breath. Surely, he's not going to pretend he hasn't seen it?

He taps on one of the apps and waits for it to load. He blinks and looks closer. 'Jesus!' He grins, showing a mouthful of white teeth, then waves his phone at his girlfriend. 'Mo, one of my vids is going off!'

'Mmhmm.' Moira taps a manicured fingernail and seems more interested in when the tea is coming. I drop a few teabags randomly into cups, keeping one ear on the conversation.

Lewis is beaming. 'This is brilliant! Wow, twenty million views! I'm TikTok famous. I knew it would happen eventually.'

I let out a gurgle of distress, which is disguised by the whistle of the kettle reaching peak boil.

'It's not you, you plonker,' says Bailey through gritted teeth. 'It's Holly. Watch it!'

Obediently, Lewis taps on the video, and I cringe as my tinny voice besmirching Christmas floats out of his phone. How many more times do I have to hear it? He watches around five seconds before thankfully shutting it off.

'I didn't post this.'

'But you did record it?' Bailey says.

'Well, yes, as a joke. We'd had a few.' His eyes shift to me, then quickly away again, almost guiltily. 'But I wouldn't post something like that. It's got nothing to do with food, and that's my theme.'

'Even if you were wasted?'

'I wasn't wasted,' scoffs Lewis, taking a seat next to Moira. She's been strangely quiet throughout Lewis's grilling, calmly waiting for her tea.

'Nice to know you were still in control of your faculties,' I say. 'I can't remember a thing since we drank practically a whole bottle of tequila.'

Moira takes a scone, splits it in half, and starts buttering it, as if she wants to move the conversation on. Lewis watches her. 'I've obviously got a stronger stomach,' he says dismissively.

'So if you didn't post it, who did?' queries Bailey, frowning.

There's a profound silence. The only sound is the ticking clock on the mantelpiece above the Aga.

Moira clears her throat, knife poised. 'Ahem. That would be me. I saw it on Lew's phone in draft and thought it was amusing. So I posted it. No harm meant.' She throws me a pleasant smile, but her eyes are steely, and I take it as a thinly veiled warning: 'Stay away from my boyfriend.'

Everything becomes much clearer, and I instantly see what's happened. Moira doesn't trust Lewis one jot. She's checked his phone at some stage after he left me, found the 'joke' TikTok, and got jealous. So she's posted it to make me look like a deranged harpy or to prove a point to him that she's got him on a short leash. I've walked into some weird power play.

Steam is starting to pour from my ears the more I stare at Moira's unrepentant face. 'Oh, lighten up, Holly. It's just a bit of fun,' she says. 'Look on the bright side—you've had your fifteen minutes of fame. Not everyone can claim that.'

Fun? Fame? My reputation is in tatters. I could lose my job. I made kids cry, and she's passing off what she did as a lark. She knew damn well what she was doing.

Moira spreads strawberry jam on the scone and adds a dollop of cream. She takes a large bite and chews contentedly. 'Mmm, delicious, Bails.' She looks at me. 'When's the tea coming?'

It's too much.

'Make your own fucking tea!' I snarl.

'Holly ...' Bailey puts a restraining hand on my arm, and I shake it off.

'Leave me alone.' I'm angry at him again too for inviting Lewis *and* Andrea and conveniently forgetting to tell me. Scones or no scones, does he even care about my feelings?

Chapter 20

If I stay in the kitchen a minute longer, I'm going to throw the kettle at Moira, and she'll end up in the serious burns unit. I need some distance. I make a lunge for the borrowed coat, shrug it on, and thrust my feet into the spare pair of wellingtons. It's time to do what I do best—make a hasty exit out the back door.

Only when I'm outside, faced with crisp air and falling snow, do I accept it may have been a hasty decision. But I'm too hopping mad to go back inside. I don't really fancy hanging out in the sheep shed. Maybe there's some kind of shelter closer to the house?

Stomping off round the side to investigate, I come across planks nailed to a trunk leading up to some kind of wooden structure—a tree house! Perfect.

Clambering up the side of a tree in wellingtons and a thick coat isn't the easiest of feats, but I somehow manage it. My head pokes up through a square hole cut in the floorboards of a small timber-lined room. It's not luxurious by any means. There are chinks in the wall, letting through a chill draft; a couple of rattan chairs with faded Pooh Bear pillows; and some tattered bunting draped along the walls. But to me, it's fantastic. I would've loved something like this growing up—a place to hide away from the world where I could read or think.

Some crayon animal drawings are still attached to the wall with yellowing Sellotape. One, a nicely drawn brown rabbit munching on an orange carrot, is signed 'BAILEY 8' in red letters. Yikes, now I'm in his childhood tree house. I can't seem to escape him. He's everywhere.

Footsteps crunch towards the base of the tree, and someone starts climbing up. I sigh in relief. He's come out looking for me. He does care. But the head that pops up through the hole isn't Bailey's—it's Kirk's. I freeze when I see his weaselly face.

'Go away.'

'Charming, especially as I come bearing gifts from your boyfriend.'

'Oh?'

He pulls himself up and sits on the edge of the hole with his legs dangling through. A red beanie is extracted out of one coat pocket—'In case you get cold'—and a buttered jammy scone wrapped in a tea towel out of the other. 'He apologises for the lack of cream but thought it would be too messy in the transportation.'

I take the offerings silently.

Kirk surveys me as I tug the beanie on. 'Are you going to sleep out here tonight then?'

'No,' I say grumpily.

'I used to on occasion, in the summer,' he says nostalgically, looking at the pictures on the wall. 'Some of those are mine. Bailey and I used to have drawing competitions. He was always better at that kind of thing. Better at most things really.'

I feel like rolling my eyes. Great, I don't really want to listen to his speech of brotherly woe.

But he changes tack. 'I know something weird is going on with you two, so you may as well spill the beans. Are you together or not?'

I heave a sigh. He may as well know. It's getting tiring trying to hide things from him. 'We weren't, but then we were. But now we aren't again. At least I think we aren't.'

'Sounds confusing.'

'Tell me about it.'

'Does it have something to do with Lewis and the TikTok?'

'We may as well get comfortable. It's a bit of a long story.'

So we sit in the rattan chairs, and I start at the beginning, telling him about meeting Bailey at the party—and how I didn't really take to him.

Kirk guffaws. 'That's a first. Everyone instantly likes him.'

'Well, I didn't. I guess because he'd overdone it on the festive clothing. He tried to make me wear the Santa hat. I don't know. It irked me.'

'He can be a little full-on, but he means well.'

Remembering it makes me feel sad. The way he looked at me with hurt puppy-dog eyes. 'Anyway, then he went off dancing with Andrea. And Lewis invited me for a nightcap, so I went with him to his hotel room. My big mistake of the evening.'

'I gather from the TikTok, it got messy.'

'Yeah.' I break off a chunk of jammy scone and stuff it in my mouth, neglecting to tell him about the drinking game. 'And it turns out he didn't even post it. Moira did. Some twisted revenge thing to get back at me when nothing even happened.'

'She didn't know that. It did look pretty dodgy.'

'I guess.'

'If that was Bailey and another woman, how would you feel?'

'I'd scratch her eyes out with a sharp pencil.'

Kirk laughs. 'You're so feisty. I can see why Bailey likes you.'

Feeling a bit better about telling him, I relay the horror

of the viral TikTok, my fleeing from Edinburgh, and bumping into Bailey in Kingussie station. 'It was the worst—my nemesis, standing right in front of me. I couldn't escape.'

Kirk snorts derisively. 'Rather dramatic.'

'Do you want to hear this or not?'

'Sorry, continue.'

'He insisted I come back with him because Crumpet needed looking after.'

'Smooth move, switching focus to the dog. Nice one, Bails.'

'Anyway', I say, ignoring him, 'your dad assumed I was his girlfriend, and he asked me to go along with it. Later, at the house, he said it was because the house was full and the only spare space was in his bedroom.'

Kirk cracks up. 'Wow, I really need to get some dating advice from him. These are great moves.'

'I assumed it was genuine,' I say stiffly. 'I don't think he was putting "the moves" on me.'

He says gently, 'Holly, you're a pretty girl—kind of angry and scary, but pretty. Of course he was putting the moves on you.'

'Oh.' That checks out with Bailey neglecting to tell me about the annexe.

'But then you left to visit Grandma?' Kirk prompts.

'Yeah. So Grandma was fictional. I'd booked a guest

house in Inverness, but it was dire. Bailey followed me and climbed into the room through the window. He thought I might have been running away from an abusive relationship.'

Kirk raises his eyebrows. 'Did you not think to tell him about the TikTok then?'

I shake my head. 'I didn't want to involve him. Then everything got muddled because now our relationship isn't pretend. It's real—for me anyway.'

I leave out the details about our night of passion.

'I'd only just relaxed about everything, but then Lewis and Moira turn up with Andrea in tow. It seems Bailey invited her but forgot ... It's all a bit much.'

I'm expecting Kirk to empathise, but he says, 'Aren't you a project manager? Bailey mentioned you were ...'

'What's that got to do with anything?'

'Well, I'm sure you have to deal with personality conflicts in your job. Can't you just manage the situation like you would at work?'

That's not a bad idea actually. I need to take a step back and view this more dispassionately. I do work with Andrea after all. Lewis is a client, and Bailey works with him. If I can see them as colleagues, then it will remove some of the angst.

'Thanks, Kirk. That's actually a great piece of

psychoanalyst advice.' I smile at him for the first time since I arrived, and he smiles back.

'Though it doesn't excuse you from showing the TikTok to the kids. That was nasty. What's your problem?'

His smile drops, and he hangs his head. 'Confession—I actually do have a therapist. I'm trying to work through some painful stuff that happened with my ex, though you're right, it doesn't excuse my behaviour. That was a dick move on my part, sorry.'

My animosity towards him lessens slightly. I get the feeling he's genuinely sorry. And don't we all have a painful past?

'It's OK. It's probably for the best that you did. Bailey had to find out at some point, and it was pretty great that he confronted Lewis ...'

All of a sudden, I really want to see him. 'Shall we go back in now? My feet are freezing.'

Kirk nods in agreement, and we climb down the tree and head back to the house. I'm about to follow him into the lounge when I see Bailey sitting next to Andrea on the couch. Moira, Lewis, Sarah, and Mirabelle are there too. They're all drinking mulled wine, chatting, and tucking into Christmas cake.

Bailey has changed into black jeans and a white shirt with the sleeves rolled up. I've never seen him wear anything but a Christmas jumper or hoodie, so I'm thrown by how hot he looks. He laughs at something Andrea says, and jealousy slices through me like a sharp steak knife. My cool, calm demeanour evaporates, and I slink back to the kitchen before he can see me.

I lean against the stone wall by the Aga, feeling the cool surface under my fingertips. *Think calming thoughts. They're just my colleagues.* But it doesn't work. I can't act impassive. He's gotten under my skin to the point I can't imagine not having him in my life. But I'm afraid I'm not good enough for him, that Andrea is a better match. Perhaps it's better to call it quits before I get hurt.

Bailey swings through the door, and I quickly swipe at my eyes. 'There you are. Are you OK? I sent Kirk out to find you.'

I paste on a smile. 'Yes, thanks for the hat, and the scone was delicious.'

He comes closer, looking a bit wary, as if I'm going to bite him. When I don't, he kisses me gently on the lips. His breath is rum-laced from the Christmas cake. He cuddles up against me and whispers in my ear, 'I missed you.' My heart melts like a marshmallow on a hot fire. I snake my arms around his warm body, unable to resist him. He's so adorable.

'Come and play Pictionary with us.'

'I don't know. What about Moira and Lewis? It'll just be awkward.'

'Everybody knows Moira posted the TikTok,' he says, nuzzling my earlobe. 'She's in the doghouse. Besides, I made Lewis delete it right after you left, so don't worry. Hollygate is over.'

A huge weight lifts off my shoulders, and I feel as light as a feather.

'Ever think about being a project manager?' I say.

In reply, Bailey smiles and gives me a deeper kiss that restores my faith. *Maybe, just maybe, I can do this.*

Chapter 21

Andrea gawps when I walk in with Bailey holding hands, and I know I'm going to have to talk to her first and explain everything.

'Do you mind if I talk to Andrea before we play?'

'Sure. How long do you need?'

'Maybe twenty?'

'OK.' He squeezes my hand.

Andrea nods when I ask her if I can talk to her. 'Let's go up to my room.'

Her *room* turns out to be a small makeshift library at the top of the house. This must be the special nook Sarah was talking about.

'This is cool,' I say, looking at the bookshelf that's been built into the eaves. It's filled with a multitude of paperbacks. There's a red beanbag, a white fluffy rug, and a mullioned window that looks out onto the snow-covered backyard with the tree house.

'Not quite what I was expecting in the way of sleeping arrangements,' Andrea says, nodding at a mattress placed on the floor with a sleeping bag and pillow.

I'm not sure I want to know what she was expecting.

'Where have they put you?' she asks.

Eek, awkward. But I can't exactly lie. 'I'm in with Bailey.'

Andrea's shoulders visibly slump, and I feel awful for her.

'I'm sorry, I know this is really weird that I'm here.'

She takes a deep breath. 'Maybe you should explain.'

I plop down into the beanbag while she sits on the mattress with her knees drawn up to her chest.

'There's not that much to tell really. I was on my way to Inverness, and the train got cancelled at Kingussie. I thought I was going to have to spend the night in the station, but Bailey happened to be there too. He convinced me to stay the night here instead, but er ... One thing led to another, and I ended up staying for Christmas. It was kind of nice actually—until Kirk played my anti-Christmas TikTok to the kids, and they freaked out.'

'Oh no! Why did he do that?'

'He didn't mean to. Well, he kind of did. But he apologised, and I've forgiven him.' *Mostly.*

'What did Bailey think about it?'

'He was more upset that I'd been carrying on with Lewis in his hotel room, which I hadn't been.'

'He must really like you,' she says softly.

I feel bad for Andrea, but she took a big risk coming here based on nothing but an invite. Unless ... I need to be brave and ask.

'Um, while I was with Lewis, did something happen with you and Bailey at the party?'

I hold my breath. This is where I find out he's been lying to me.

'Not really. Not like that. I guess I just got my hopes up. We were having fun, and when he was talking about Lewis coming here, he invited me too. I jumped at the chance to get to know him better.'

'And then I got in first.'

'It's OK. I don't hold it against you. He's a lovely guy. I just didn't think you liked him.'

'Neither did I. It's been a trial by fire, especially as he's so into Christmas.' I pull a face, and she laughs.

'I'm glad that awful TikTok got sorted out. What a nightmare for you, bloody Moira.'

'Do you think Valerie saw it?'

'Hopefully not. I'll let you know if Melanie says anything to me.'

There's a silence as we both look at our respective laps.

'So are you and Bailey officially a couple then?' Andrea asks eventually.

I shrug. 'I'm definitely his elf girlfriend. Beyond that, I

don't know. It hasn't been discussed. It's all moving quite fast.'

'His "*elf* girlfriend"? Don't tell me he got you to dress up?'

I nod sheepishly.

'And you enjoyed yourself?'

I nod again, my face burning.

Andrea's mouth forms an O. 'Holly Driver, this is monumental.'

I cover my eyes with my hands. 'I know, I know.'

Sarah and Mirabelle are setting up the board when we come down. The other Pictionary players are Moira, Lewis, and Kirk. We're playing in teams of two, and Kirk seems happy about teaming up with Andrea, but I can tell she isn't. I don't blame her. It's taken me a while to get the hang of him, but I've concluded he's not a bad guy—just damaged goods like me.

'How does this work?' I ask, realising I don't actually know the rules.

'You've never played Pictionary?' Moira is astounded.

I shake my head.

Bailey explains, 'Basically, the aim is to guess the word the other person draws within one minute. The first team to reach the finish square wins. There are other minor rules, but I'll tell you as we go along.'

'Just warning you: I can only draw stick figures,' I say worriedly, hoping Bailey doesn't expect me to be Leonardo da Vinci or anything.

'That's OK. That's what makes it fun ...' He lowers his voice and whispers, 'You're on the winning team. I'm an excellent drawer.'

'I know, I saw your bunny rabbit,' I whisper back.

He looks confused. 'My what?'

'In the tree house. On the wall.'

'Oh, that. I've improved a million times since then.'

'It's not an art competition,' says Kirk to my right, overhearing our conversation. 'You've got to be in sync with the other person.' He smiles at Andrea, but she remains tight-lipped. Oh dear.

The game commences.

Lewis and Moira go first. Lewis shakes the dice and moves their red counter onto a blue square, which means it's an object apparently. When the hourglass timer is turned over, he draws a round circle and then looks at her. 'Circle,' says Moira confidently. Lewis shakes his head and draws another heavier circle round the first one. 'Stone?' Another head shake.

'Ring?' More head shakes.

Lewis just keeps helplessly drawing circles as the sand in

the hourglass timer runs down. Moira starts panicking. 'Er ... um ...' The sand runs out.

'It was a well!' exclaims Lewis.

'Jesus, you could've drawn something else to indicate that,' Moira says, sounding annoyed. 'Like a bucket or something.'

'True,' admits Lewis. 'My bad.'

OK, so you have to think laterally; and the more synonyms you know, the better.

We're up next.

Bailey shakes the dice and moves our yellow counter onto a green square. He looks at the card, and when the timer is turned over, he quickly starts drawing a round shape with a trunk.

'Elephant,' I say.

Bailey shakes his head and draws a tusk.

'Tusk!' Another shake.

He draws a violent slash through the elephant's body. OK, that got dark quickly.

'Death! Kill! Poacher! Elephant graveyard!' I cry.

'Time's nearly up,' says Kirk. Shit. I'm letting the side down.

Bailey draws more arrows to the tusk frantically.

Duh, of course! 'Ivory!' I screech just before the last grains of sand disappear.

'Boo-yah!' Bailey throws down his pencil and grins at me triumphantly. 'Great work, team!'

I quietly congratulate myself.

'Holly, you get to go now,' says Kirk.

'Oh, right.'

My stomach churns as I roll the dice. Hopefully, Bailey can guess the word. My drawing skills are so bad. We land on a blue square, so it's an object. I glance at the card to see my word. Kirk flips over the hourglass before I have a chance to think too much about it. Quickly, I write the number 1 and draw a door with lines radiating around it and a stick person with their hand on the knob. Then I write the number 2 and draw a cock and balls.

Laughter erupts around the coffee table.

'It's too big for Bailey's!' hoots Lewis.

Ignoring him, I draw an arrow to the cock part.

Bailey is looking highly amused. God knows what he's thinking. But to me, the word is pretty obvious. I wait as he mutters various word combinations under his breath: 'Door cock?' 'Person penis?' 'Shut cock?' Then he yells, 'Shuttlecock!'

'Yup!' I show him and everyone else the card.

Bailey whoops in glee. 'That was really clever, Holly! I love you so much right now,' he says, popping the card at the back of the pile. 'Our turn again.'

My heart skitters sideways. Did he just say 'I love you' in front of everyone?

Bailey busily rolls the dice while Moira mutters under her breath, 'She could've just drawn a shuttlecock and a badminton net.'

I try not to react outwardly, but inside, I'm awash with different emotions. Surely, it was just a throwaway comment? Nothing to get worked up about. Bailey's just absurdly competitive when it comes to board games. He'd say that to anyone if he was winning. But I notice Sarah is smiling broadly. She gives me a sly wink, as if to say 'You're in there, girl. Just don't fuck it up'.

Chapter 22

By the time the evening rolls around, I've decided Bailey being in love with me is ridiculous. We hardly know each other. It's based on oxytocin, nothing more. I'm tempted to just brush what he said under my emotional carpet. There's already a lot of other junk under there, so one more ambiguity won't matter.

But it still niggles. He can't just say stuff like that without me questioning it. Why shouldn't I ask for clarification if I'm unsure what's happening with us? Kirk's suggestion that I take more control of the situation resonates with me. Why not apply it to this? I need to start taking emotional responsibility rather than just blindly accepting my fate. I'm not a child anymore. I do have some power over my life—why not state plainly and firmly what I want?

So when Bailey and I are in bed, I gently float the subject of *us*.

'What happens when we go back to Edinburgh?'

He doesn't answer for a bit. 'Work, I guess. I'm rostered on at the hotel for New Year's. How long have you got off?'

'Just until after New Year's.'

'We'd better make the most of it then,' he says, rolling towards me.

I place a hand on his chest. 'Bailey ...'

'What?'

I struggle to find the right words. 'Um, I kind of need to know where this is going.'

Yikes, that sounds like I'm thinking about marriage and kids. I back-pedal quickly. 'I mean, should I be handing in the notice on my flat?'

Shit, that's worse! Now it sounds like I want to live with him.

'I really like you,' says Bailey slowly. I wait for him to elaborate, but that seems to be it. An awkward silence brews, and tension builds in my chest as I realise that this might only be a Christmas fling.

'I thought ... what you said during Pictionary.'

'What did I say?' He sounds genuinely confused. 'Sorry, I've got a crap memory at the best of times. Remind me.'

'Ah, that's cool,' I mumble.

'Maybe we both need some time to think about what we want?' he says with a yawn. 'We can talk in the morning?'

'Sure.' I turn over and lie there, rigid, with blood pounding in my ears. Oh my god, it *was* just a throwaway comment. Thank fuck I didn't state plainly and firmly what

I want. He would've shot me down in flames!

Our conversation keeps me lying awake for hours, blinking in the darkness. If I had my way, I'd silently pack up my stuff, nudge Crumpet awake, creep downstairs, and be out the front door so fast I'd only be a memory.

But I'm in the middle of nowhere.

It's an hour's drive to the nearest train station.

And it's winter.

If I were Bear Grylls, I'd probably make it on foot, but I'm not. Someone's going to have to drive me to the station. Either Bailey, his dad, or Lewis. Out of the three, his dad is the safest option. All that remains now is to broach the subject with Bailey and come up with a believable excuse as to why I'm leaving on his birthday. Strangely enough, now that I've made the decision to go home, I fall into a peaceful sleep.

I wake from something solid pressing against me. One of Bailey's arms is flung over my hip, and he's snuggled up against me. *Probably only to keep warm*, I think cynically.

I'm under no illusion that what's going on is the love affair to end all love affairs. I've just been a project for him to work on—something to fix, like the owl with a broken wing. Well, I'm not going to hop around after him like a pathetic creature desperate for his love. I lift his arm off me, slide out from under the covers, and quickly get dressed in jeans and a warm jumper. Crumpet looks up at me and wags his tail.

'We're leaving, buddy, and not a moment too soon,' I whisper to him.

I'm tiptoeing around, picking up items of clothing, and packing my bag as silently as I can when there's a sleepy grunt of someone waking up behind me.

Bailey's sleep-filled voice sounds in the darkness. 'What are you doing?'

Ooops. 'Er, packing.'

'What for? It's bloody early. Come back to bed.'

'I think I'm going to go home actually. Do you think your dad could drive me to the station this morning?'

That pours cold water on him. Bailey sits up in bed and switches on the bedside light. He's wearing a blue T-shirt with 'Merry Christmas' and a family of dancing gingerbread men on it. He peers at me blearily. 'Is this about what we discussed last night?'

'It wasn't much of a discussion.'

He pats the side of the bed. 'Sit down.'

I sit.

'Why don't you tell me what you want out of this?'

If Kirk was here, I know exactly what he'd say: 'Ho ho ho. Nice move, Bails. Get her to go first.'

Fine, if he wants to know. 'I'm willing to rethink my self-imposed single status for you,' I say formally.

Bailey looks amused. 'You make it sound like going out with me would be a prison sentence.'

I lift my chin. 'What about you?'

'I haven't really thought about it.'

I look at him, aghast. 'You haven't?'

'Not really. I was just living in the moment.'

I groan inwardly, feeling tricked into revealing too much. He really is the worst.

'You're a man-child,' I say, my voice wavering.

'That's unfair.'

'It's true. You're living in some Christmas fairy-tale bubble. It's not reality.'

'I wasn't aware I was doing that ...'

'You have no idea what it's like to grow up feeling unwanted and unloved.'

Bailey purses his lips and looks at me with what I judge to be pity.

'You're right, I don't. I have to wonder, though. Is it me you want or my family?'

I open my mouth and shut it again. I can't deny Bailey's awesome family is a powerful drawcard. Would I want him if he didn't come with that?

He sighs wearily. 'If you really want to go home, I'll ask

Dad to drive you to the station. Stay for breakfast at least. I'm making my famous birthday pancakes.'

Shit, I forgot. 'Happy birthday,' I squeak guiltily. 'You shouldn't have to cook, though.'

'Speaking of reality, Holly, this is mine. When you're a chef, you cook—even when it's your birthday.'

Touché. I didn't really think of it like that. I guess he doesn't have the luxury of someone cooking him a meal. Everyone's always enjoying the fruits of his labour because he's so good at it.

'I'll make them,' I say quickly.

'You don't have to.'

'No, I want to. To say thanks for having me.' *Before I leave in a cloud of dust without looking back.*

Full of purpose, I pad downstairs and flick on the lights. It's so early no one else is up yet. I bring up some recipe options on my phone, looking for something with a bit of pizzazz. Not that I'm trying to impress Bailey with my cooking skills, of course. I've neglected to tell him I've never cooked pancakes before, but how hard can it be? I google 'fancy breakfast pancakes', and photos of pancake animals appear. There's an owl, a lion, a teddy bear, and a reindeer. He would *love* that! It seems quite easy—just make different-sized pancake rounds for the heads and ears and decorate them with fruit. Easy-peasy.

First, ingredients: flour, milk, salt, sugar, baking powder, eggs, butter. Check.

Second, fruit for decorations: bananas, apples, raspberries, and there's even chocolate buttons. Check.

Hmm, there are quite a lot of people to cook for, so I probably need to double or triple the basic recipe I've found.

Donning my candy cane apron, I eye the Aga. Luckily, it's a gas cooker, so it should be pretty easy to fire up. This really cannot go wrong.

Right, the batter is mixed. There seems to be an awful lot of it. How many pancakes is this going to make? I brush aside my sudden doubt. They'll be so delicious everyone will have second helpings.

I chuck a knob of butter in a cast-iron frying pan, and it melts. All that's left to do is to pour in some batter, wait for it to cook, and flip the pancake. My first attempt is half-baked mush that breaks into pieces. That hurriedly gets put in the bin. Maybe I should turn the heat up? Butter is now sizzling. Pour, wait, and flip. But I wait too long, and its bottom is burnt. Gosh, this Aga doesn't have any middle ground. This is going to be tricky. That one goes in the bin too.

I google 'how to fix your pancake problem'. Luckily, there's an in-depth article on it. The article suggests adding more flour and waiting for bubbles to appear before flipping. This time, I get it right. The perfect pancake! Phew.

Each animal has, on average, four different-sized pancakes. So if there's seventeen people (not counting baby Eve), I just have to do sixty-seven more. I wipe my damp brow with my hand, feeling slightly panicked. It's too late now. I'm committed.

Who knew pancakes would be so bloody difficult? This bitch of an Aga isn't my friend, and I'm sweating madly from the heat and the exertion of trying to flip pancakes with ease and agility. I assumed the more pancakes I made, the better I would get. But that isn't the case. I've used nearly a whole pat of butter to grease the pan, and there are more pancakes in the bin than on the plate. Dollops of pancake batter are all over the Aga. I need to clean that up before it bakes hard.

I'm on the verge of giving up when the door opens, and in comes Bailey. He's still wearing his blue gingerbread T-shirt, but he's pulled on a pair of grey jogging bottoms. The front lock of his hair sticks up adorably like Tintin's.

'Whoa,' he says, surveying the state of the Aga.

'I'm going to clean it up,' I say tearfully.

He comes over and gently steers me towards the kitchen table. 'You've done really well so far. Maybe have a seat for a bit.'

'But I'm supposed to be making them for you.' I show him the photo on my phone.

'Cute idea. I'm just going to *assist* a little.'

'Well, OK,' I say. *Thank God he's taking over.*

'Why don't you chop the fruit?'

I halve an apple and watch as he checks the consistency of the batter.

'This is good,' he says. Hah, I knew I was doing something right.

He adjusts the temperature of the Aga and pours in some batter, tilts the pan to spread the batter evenly, and then expertly flips them. Soon, there's a mound of fluffy golden pancakes on the plate, covering my pitiful attempts.

'You need smaller ones for the eyes and mouths,' I tell him, busily slicing bananas.

Bailey obediently cooks a bunch of smaller ones.

Then we assemble the animals and scrape off the pancake batter splattered on the Aga. I expect him to make a joke about it, but he doesn't.

We've just finished when the kitchen door opens, and Susie and Sasha wander in, dressed in matching pink PJs. Then they see the pancakes. Susie squeals, 'I want the teddy bear!' The commotion brings in the rest of the kids, and soon, there's a pancake party going on at the table.

Then Jennifer appears in her purple dressing gown.

'What's happening?' she asks.

'Holly made animal pancakes for my birthday,' says Bailey with a smile at me. 'Dig in. There's plenty.'

'How lovely,' she says, giving her son a hug. 'Happy birthday, darling. Holly, there's some maple syrup in the pantry if you want to grab it.'

I nod and head off to the pantry, but Bailey follows and corners me before I can escape.

'Thanks for taking over,' I say, lowering my eyes. 'That went better in my head.'

'No problem. So are you staying then?'

I shake my head. 'I think this thing—whatever it is—has reached its natural conclusion.'

'Oh.' He looks mildly surprised, as if he thought our pancake making had somehow erased the previous conversation.

'It's for the best.'

Bailey gazes at me, expressionless. Is he angry? Sad? I can't read him.

'Sorry about the timing.'

He turns to leave. 'Don't worry about it. There'll be other birthdays.'

And I take that to mean 'without you'.

Chapter 23

The story that I'm telling everyone is that I stupidly booked my return ticket for today instead of tomorrow, and I can't change it or cancel it to get a refund, which is partly true. I do have a return ticket for today. I bought it immediately after I booked the Inverness guest house on the train coming up here. But the rest is a flimsy excuse, and I'm not sure people are buying it. Kirk definitely isn't now that he knows the whole sorry story.

'But it's Bailey's birthday. You can't go today.' I take heart in Sarah being genuinely disappointed I'm leaving. She helps me bring my bag downstairs and out to the waiting car Allan has just brought around.

'We'll go out for dinner when he gets back to Edinburgh,' I fib.

'Oooh yes, so he doesn't have to cook. And you'll have to come to London and visit us soon too.'

I make a non-committal noise of agreement.

Bailey hasn't been seen since our conversation in the pantry. I'm sure by now he's come to the same conclusion I have—that there's no point in taking this any further. Our backgrounds are too different. He's probably regretting even starting anything with me since I'm a basket case.

I'm just about to get into the car when he comes dashing out at the last minute, clutching the green tinsel bow. He fastens it onto Crumpet's collar, who's jumped up at him, wagging his tail.

I narrow my eyes. *Cute, very cute, but that can come off.* The Christmas fairy tale is over, and I'm heading back to real life, where there aren't any sparkles.

'Just leave it on until you get home,' he says, as if he knows what I'm thinking. 'Might help you strike up a conversation on the train.'

Wow, he's encouraging me to meet other guys already!

I shrug. 'Fine.'

Bailey leans down and kisses me on the cheek. 'Keep in touch,' he mutters while I try not to flinch as his familiar spicy scent invades my nostrils and makes my head swim. Well, I guess he has to say something in front of Sarah, Jennifer, and Kirk—the McAdams family members who've come outside to see me off. Lewis, Moira, and Andrea are still in bed. Knowing that Bailey is going to be spending his birthday with Andrea, and they could feasibly get together, is a bitter pill to swallow. But logically, I can see she's a better choice for him—less trouble all round.

I feign a smile. Friends it is. I guess that's better than

nothing. But I'm not sure even that will happen since he still hasn't given me his number.

'Bye ...' He waits until the car moves off before loping off into the house without looking back. Well, OK, that's it, I guess.

The ensuing surge of emotion at his nonchalance hits me by surprise, and I give myself a strong talking-to as we head towards the entranceway. My heart feels like it's being stabbed with a fondue fork. Making small talk with Allan while fighting back tears isn't easy either. My replies either come out as guinea pig grunts, or I give erratic head nods. It's the longest hour of my life.

At the station, Allan hands me my bag. 'It's been so great to spend time with you, Holly. And I hope you're all right about that TikTok nonsense. Just put it out of your mind. We certainly have.' He gives me one of his famous bear hugs as a parting gesture.

I swallow hard so I don't burst into tears and do another erratic head nod against his chest.

'Hopefully, we see you when we pop down to Edinburgh in the new year for a visit,' he says.

'Sounds awesome! Thanks so much for the lift, Allan!' I guinea pig squeal, and Crumpet and I trot off into the station as fast as our legs can carry us.

Inside, I breathe a huge sigh of relief. It's over. The

weirdest Christmas I've ever had in my life is finally over! Maybe next year, I will go to London. Christmas with my foster family is awful, but at least it's predictably awful.

When I arrive back at my flat after the four-hour train journey, it's dark as night even though it's only early afternoon. I flick on the lights and stand in the lounge with my bag, feeling disorientated. Crumpet runs around, sniffing all the furniture. Shaking myself out of my reverie, I do the human version of reacquainting with my home: unpacking.

The flat still shows signs of my hurried departure before Christmas. There's a mess of clothing on my bed from the flurry of last-minute packing. An upturned water glass on the kitchen counter reminds me of rehydrating madly after the night of tequila drinking. Thankfully, the horror of the TikTok has faded at last, and I'm praying I don't have any blowback from it. The last thing I need now is to get fired, especially after I managed to get a love life, then somehow lost it.

Crumpet pads past and dips his head to lap from the water bowl I've just filled. The green tinsel bow on his collar glistens, and I know I should remove it, but I can't make myself. Bailey put it there, and it's my only reminder of him.

Why did it all go so wrong?

Just because I asked what was going on?

I obviously opened a can of worms with my question, but it was still the right decision to clarify things. I'm glad I did. At least I know there's not going to be an *us*, so I'm saved from waiting around and hoping.

It's an effort, but I force myself to visit the local Tesco and buy some groceries, a few things to tide me over until I'm in a better state of mind to order a larger shop. I walk around the store like I'm an alien dropped in from another planet. But once I've heated up some tomato soup, buttered some toast, and turned on the telly, I start to feel human again. After a few good nights' sleep, I'm sure I'll be back to normal in no time.

But that night, I have a dream or, should I say, a vision because it's so real. Bailey and I are in the tree house, and we're sitting in the rattan chairs. I'm telling him how I'm stuck in a rut and don't know what to do. Bailey's wearing those ridiculous elf ears and appears to be listening intently. With a serene expression on his face, he smiles and says, 'Holly, you can do anything you put your mind to. We believe in you.'

I wake with a start, hollow despair in the pit of my stomach, knowing I'm never going to see him again. Why couldn't I just go with the flow and keep my big mouth shut? Now he's probably lying in bed with his arms around Andrea after an evening of birthday cake and whisky nightcaps. I cry myself back to sleep with bitter tears of self-loathing.

However, in the morning, I feel better. Crumpet jumps up on my bed and snuggles in. I breathe deeply. I'm OK. Everything's OK. No one's died. Perhaps Bailey and I weren't meant to be together, but there's a lesson I can take away from the dream. There are people out there willing to believe in me, even when I am at my worst. Maybe I can turn the TikTok experience around and have something good come out of it? Make lemonade out of lemons, as they say? Suddenly, an idea pops into my brain. I know exactly what I'm going to do.

Later that day

I adjust my phone to make sure I'm in frame. I'm wearing the black dress with batwing sleeves from the party to remind people of who I am. The account name I've set up is @UnjollyHolly.

This is my third attempt at recording a TikTok, and I'm beginning to wish I had some tequila stashed in the cupboard for Dutch courage. But no, I have to do this sober, or no one's going to take me seriously. I just need to relax and be myself.

Pushing the round red 'record' button, I straighten my

shoulders and smile. 'Hey, so you may have seen my anti-Christmas rant, which has been doing the rounds on TikTok. I just want to come on and say yes, I hate the commercialism of Christmas. But even more, I hate what we're doing to the planet. I'm a project manager who's been working on a sustainability initiative with a local Edinburgh hotel, so I thought it would be cool to give some insights into that. For instance, did you know the duvet inner I was sitting on in that video is made from recycled plastic bottles? How crazy is that? There are more eco-friendly changes happening around the city too, some of which may surprise you. So stay tuned!'

With a shaking finger, I press the 'stop recording' button. Whoa, I think that's the one. I watch it back, and it's fine. Casual, relaxed, not too frowny. There's something to be said for being in control and not wearing a shower cap or wielding a hairdryer. Eat your heart out, Greta Thunberg.

I should probably get the OK from Lewis before I talk more about what they're doing. But I can't foresee a problem. I'm not muscling in on his personal foodie vids. His hotel is going to get exposure, and well ... he owes me.

Even if I don't get loads of followers, views, or comments, it just feels good to be doing something positive and be known for something other than a grinch. I don't want to be remembered for that.

As I'm a new account, TikTok gives my video a special push to start me off. Within an hour, I'm up to 500 views, ten likes, twelve followers, and three comments:

Climate change sux! Eggnog is the worst!

Just followed! Love your vibe.

You're raw and real and I relate so much!

Harmony washes over me. People are responding and resonating in a good way. I'm not a social pariah. This could actually be fun.

Another comment pops up:

Nice dress, where did you buy pls?

Chapter 24

I've been home a few days and moping around when Andrea messages: *I'm back in Ed. Are you going to the NYE thing at the hotel?*

I'm not sure what to say to that. Finally, I type, *I haven't been invited.*

Andrea immediately rings.

'Hi, I thought Bailey would have?'

My heart sinks like a stone. 'Nope.'

'Oh, it probably slipped his mind. Well, you should definitely come. It's starting at ten. There's a rooftop terrace to watch the fireworks and a few drinks. Nothing full-on.'

'Maybe.' Yeah, like that's going to happen. There's no way I'm going to put myself out there again. Besides, I've got my evening planned already: a heat-and-eat lasagne, a glass of red wine, and a movie with Crumpet. I'll probably be in bed asleep by ten.

I wrestle between the curiosity to know what went on at the house and to remain aloof. Curiosity wins. 'So what happened after I left?'

'Nothing too much. We visited Ballindalloch Distillery.

Bailey made a cake. We played charades and then had a nice dinner. We left the next day. Lewis and Bailey had to get back to the hotel to plan for New Year's Eve.'

'How was he?'

'Who? Bailey?'

'Yes.'

'Missing you.'

My heart floats to the ceiling like a helium balloon and bobs around up by the cornicing. 'Really? What makes you say that?' I hate the eagerness in my voice. *Tone it down, Holly.*

'He was moping around like a lost puppy. I'm glad for you, by the way.'

'Don't be,' I say, deflating my own hope balloon. 'Nothing's going on.'

'But I thought ...?'

'It's not going to work.'

'Oh, are you sure? I got the impression he's really into you.'

As much as I want to believe that, I can't. From the way he scooted into the house, Bailey couldn't wait to escape my company. Nothing seems to have happened with Andrea, though. Strange.

I grunt in reply, but Andrea doesn't seem to hear.

'It's funny, I went up there with the intention of getting

to know Bailey, but I ended up liking his brother.'

'What? But Simon's married!' I exclaim, aghast. How could she?

'No, not Simon, you dummy! Kirk.'

'Kirk?'

'Yes, I wasn't too sure about him at first. But once we got to chatting, I discovered we had a lot in common, and he's pretty cute.'

If you like the weaselly look, I think but then feel bad. Kirk is OK.

'I know what you mean. He's got layers, like an onion. They just need peeling back.'

Andrea giggles. 'I'm happy to oblige.'

'Urgh, too much information.'

'Come tomorrow night pleeeaaase. Bailey will be busy in the kitchen, so you won't even see him if you don't want to. You can chat to me and Kirk. He's coming over from Glasgow.'

In the spirit of the new sociable Holly, I should probably go. Plus I can take some video footage of the hotel for TikTok. And if Bailey won't actually be around ...

'I'll think about it,' I say. 'I'll let you know.'

I think about (or, should I say, overanalyse) it too much for my own good—wobbling backwards and forwards, writing lists of pros and cons.

On the afternoon of New Year's Eve, I still haven't decided. It feels weird to turn up on an invite from Andrea rather than Bailey. I'm just about to toss a coin—heads, I go; tails, I stay—when I notice Crumpet pawing at the tinsel bow. It's annoying him. It's annoying me too having to look at it.

'Come here, mate.'

Crumpet leaps up onto the couch, and I unwind the tinsel from his collar. When I reach the end, there's a folded bit of paper. It's been tucked up underneath the collar, out of sight. Gingerly, I open it, hardly daring to breathe. It says,

Hi Holly,

I know you hate parties but we're having drinks on the rooftop terrace for Hogmanay. It would be great to see you there. Come at 10pm if you're free.

Bailey x

My heart fills with joy, sails out the window and into the sky before I can rein it in. I know I shouldn't get my hopes up. Although he has put a kiss at the end of the note, it could just be a friendly invite. This is Bailey. I could turn up, and he might have forgotten he even invited me.

Quickly, I message Andrea: *I'm coming to the NYE thing.* She replies with *Great!* and a thumbs up.

I'm quivering with anticipation at seeing Bailey again. Throwing open my wardrobe, I rifle through my clothes. Everything's so dull and boring even amongst what is stuffed in the back.

I message Andrea again: *Hi, do you have anything I can wear? I only have the black dress and I don't want to wear that again.*

Almost as if she's been waiting for it, she messages back instantly: *What's your address? I'll come over after dinner with some options. We can go together Ax*

I heave a sigh of relief: *Thanks that would be good Hx*

We catch an Uber to the hotel at 9.45 p.m. As we turn into the hotel's street, I get an attack of nerves. What I'm wearing suddenly feels too tight, too short, and too showy. My stomach flops around like a half-dead fish on a pier, and my vision blurs. 'I think I'm going to be sick,' I gasp.

Uber driver Mick hears and touches the brakes. 'I'll pull over.'

Andrea pushes my head down between my legs. 'No, carry on. She hasn't been drinking. It's just a nervous stomach.'

'If she does, I'm charging you for the clean,' he grumbles.

'She won't,' says Andrea. I'm not sure why she's so confident. I'm really not well. I shouldn't have even come out. This was a mistake. I haven't even had a proper dinner. She said there was going to be food, so I just made us some cheese and crackers.

Thanks to Andrea whispering words of encouragement, when we arrive at the hotel, I extract myself from the car vomit-free. The glass façade of the hotel rears above us. The lobby lights are welcoming, but there isn't a steady stream of raucous guests entering through the double doors.

'Are you sure there's a party on? It looks dead.'

'It's sort of a private function.'

'Oh.' My nerves return full force. Is Bailey going to be mingling with the guests, handing out hors d'oeuvres?

We step into the lift, and Andrea pushes the button labelled 'roof terrace'. But when the lift doors open, the terrace itself is cold and dark. However, the lights of the city do look pretty from up here.

'Are we too early?' I ask, shivering in my coat as a gust of icy wind blasts across the rooftop. 'There's no one here.'

Then a figure looms in front of me, and I let out a screech until I see its face. Bailey.

'Hey, it's just me,' he says.

'That's my cue,' says Andrea with a smile, stepping back

into the lift. 'Have a great night, you guys, and happy New Year.' She blows a kiss. The doors close on her, and she's gone. I blink.

'She's off to meet Kirk,' says Bailey, anticipating my question. 'His mate is having a party in Haymarket.'

'But ...' I look around, confused, expecting more people to jump out of the shadows.

'I asked her for help getting you here. I was worried you wouldn't come.'

'What's going on?'

'Walk this way, and you'll see.' Bailey beckons for me to follow him around the side of the lift shaft. Only then do I see he's dressed in full Scottish regalia: a black jacket with gold buttons, a white shirt with black bow tie, and a kilt with the McAdams family tartan—complete with knee-length black socks and shoes. He even has a furry sporran. Good lord! Hogmanay just got traditional. Maybe he's part of a bagpipe performance before the fireworks? But no one at Christmas mentioned he played them.

There are no other bagpipers around the corner. Instead, there is a sheltered nook right in view of the castle. There's a square of artificial grass, and on it is a couch with a fluffy throw. A couple of heat lamps at either end of the couch are glowing in a toasty fashion. In front of the couch, a low table holds a grazing platter of breads, dips, mini pizzas, quiche, and chocolate strawberries. There's a bucket of ice with champagne and a bottle of red wine.

I suck in a breath of frosty air as I realise what's happening. It's a private function all right—it's just for me!

'You didn't have much to eat before you came, did you?' Bailey asks worriedly.

I shake my head dazedly.

'Do you want to take off your coat and sit down?' Wondering if I'm in a dream, I hand over my coat to him and plop down onto one end of the couch. 'You look amazing, by the way.'

'Thanks.' I tug down the hem of Andrea's sparkly white minidress, which I've paired with black-and-white polka-dot tights and black combat boots. 'I feel a bit underdressed with you in your kilt.'

'At least your tights cover your knees,' Bailey replies, hanging up my coat on a nearby coatrack. He's thought of everything.

'Come to think of it, yours do look a bit blue.' I check him out surreptitiously. Bailey can certainly pull off the kilt look. A ripple of desire runs through my body. I wonder if he's wearing underwear or not—and if I'm going to find out.

I clear my throat. 'You look great, though. So I thought there were going to be more people at this party?'

Bailey sits next to me and gestures at the wine, and I nod.

'No, it's just us. Are you disappointed?' He unscrews the cap and pours me a glass. I take a sip and lean back against the couch, feeling more relaxed than I have in days. My nerves seem to have disappeared entirely now that I know what's going on—I'm being wooed by a hot Scotsman in a kilt. I'm glad I got dolled up after all.

I shake my head. 'Relieved actually.'

'I figured.' Bailey takes a long swallow of wine. He seems to be more nervous than I am.

'This is ...' I take a deep breath. 'Lovely. Really lovely of you. I can't believe you'd do this after I left on your birthday. I thought that was it, that I'd ruined things.'

He shakes his head. 'I handled that badly. I'm sorry. You took me by surprise. I knew I wanted more, but I just hadn't thought about the logistics.'

'Logistics?'

'As in I want to go on dates with you, get to know you better, have you stay over at my flat or stay at yours. And if we don't see eye to eye, I want to argue with you. And if that doesn't work, beat you with a cushion and then have make-up sex,' he blurts in a rush.

I laugh out loud. 'That sounds like my kind of relationship.'

'Really?'

'Of course. There's nothing I'd like more than to beat you with a cushion, especially if you're wearing a googly-eyed Christmas jumper.'

Bailey grins, flashing his dimples, and I practically melt. 'I missed you as soon as I went inside the house.'

'I missed you the moment we drove off.'

He rolls his eyes and laughs. 'What a pair. Now, not to change the subject, but can I interest you in a piece of quiche, madam?'

'Only if you tell me what you're wearing underneath your kilt.' *Holly Driver, you are a brazen hussy, and you've hardly even had a drop of wine.* But I don't care. It's the end of the old me and the start of the new.

And by the way, Bailey takes my hand and slides it slowly up his thigh—it's not quiche he's trying to interest me in.

At ten to midnight, we're munching away hungrily on the spread, having worked up a bit of an appetite.

'Thanks for doing so much food,' I say, taking a large bite of a mini pizza. 'Carrot sticks and hummus wouldn't have cut it.'

'My pleasure. Or, should I say, *yours*,' says Bailey with a wicked glint in his eye.

I give him a nudge. 'It's not my fault you showed up in a

kilt. What did you expect?'

He chuckles. 'Well, I was wearing it for the dinner service, and I hoped you might be turned on by it. I didn't think it would work that well, though.'

I smooth my hair, which has frizzed from our frenzied make-out session on the couch. This has been quite the turn of events. 'I think if you were wearing a reindeer onesie, I still would've flung myself on you,' I say, blushing.

Bailey smiles and dunks a piece of bread into some dip. 'So I take it we're "real dating" now?'

'Yes, if you really want me,' I say, feeling uncertain again and needing his reassurance. He takes my hand and kisses it.

'I want you. I pretty much knew when I first saw you that I wanted you. Even though you hated my guts.'

I stifle a laugh. 'I didn't! Well, maybe a bit. How was I to know plonking a Santa hat on my head was you trying to make a move?'

'Hmm, let's forget that, how do you feel about me now?' Bailey asks before taking a bite of his bread.

That's easy. 'I wanted you from the moment you climbed through the window of that shitty guest house in Inverness. I just didn't know how to ask for it in case ... in case I'm not what you're looking for.'

Bailey looks at me enquiringly. 'What do you mean?'

'I mean—to put it bluntly—I'm fucked up.'

'We're all fucked up,' he says, softly rubbing his thumb across the back of my hand. I stare at the castle, feeling cold all of a sudden despite the heat from the lamps.

'Some of us more than others.'

'You're not your foster family.'

'No, but you'll have to meet them at some point. You might want to get out now while you have the chance.'

Bailey laughs. 'How bad can they be?'

I shrug. 'I guess you'll find out.'

Before he can ask me any probing questions about that, there's a boom, and a series of explosions burst over our heads. Bailey checks his watch. 'Shit, I was meant to count down. It's midnight!'

He pops the champagne; and I stare upwards, mesmerised as the sky rains green, red, and blue stars. I feel happy, hopeful, and absolutely stuffed to the gills from eating five mini pizzas.

I look round to find Bailey gazing at me, the lights from the fireworks reflecting in his eyes. I brush his hair from his forehead and kiss him gently on the lips. 'Happy New Year. Here's looking to the future and not the past.'

He nods and hands me a slim glass of golden fizz. 'I'll drink to that.'

With our glasses of champers, we snuggle up on the couch under the fluffy throw to watch the rest of the fireworks. It's pure bliss.

'So you'll still want me even if I'm in grinch mode?' I joke. 'It's not always going to be champagne and fireworks, you know.'

'I can handle Unjolly Holly and her climate change rants.'

I stiffen under the throw. 'How do you know about that?'

'Lewis may have mentioned that you'd been in touch about featuring the hotel in some eco-friendly TikToks.'

'Ah, yes.'

'I think it's a good idea. Let me know if you need any help with footage. We've been implementing some new measures in the kitchen to do with food waste.'

'Sounds good. I'll schedule you in for a filming.' I stroke his bare knee. 'I don't suppose you'd wear the kilt for it ...'

Bailey rolls his eyes. 'What have I started?'

I just smile and clink my glass to his, 'Sláinte.'

It's a brand-new year—a clean slate, if you will. And with Bailey by my side (whether he's wearing a kilt, a Christmas jumper or his birthday suit), I have a feeling it's going to be the best year of my life.

Chapter 25

One year later

'Are you ready?' Bailey calls from the lounge, where he's been setting up his laptop on the coffee table.

'As ready as I'll ever be,' I mutter in the bedroom. I've made a start on packing, which isn't really necessary since we're not leaving until noon. It's just to distract myself. I don't really want to have this Zoom call with my foster family, but Bailey suggested it since we're not going down to London for Christmas this year—or any year if I have my way. But I'm trying to be amenable.

'Come on, it's nearly ten.'

When I walk in, he's sitting on the couch, logging in to Zoom. I sigh and plonk down next to him. *Think happy thoughts. Think happy thoughts.* That's not too hard to do actually. Life with Bailey during the past year has been incredible. He's incredible. I feel like a brand new, happier version of myself thanks to his steady TLC and the support of his loving family.

Sometimes I catch Crumpet looking at me as if to say 'who is this girl?'

We're now living together in my flat since he was renting in New Town and the trek over to Old Town every second day was getting annoying. It makes sense financially too. Why pay rent on two flats when we're practically joined at the hip? That's not a commentary on our sex life either. Bailey's hours are unsociable, but we've managed to fit in around each other to make sure we spend quality time together.

Of course, there are days when I want to strangle Bailey with my two bare hands but after a McAdams tartan cushion fight to let off steam, I'm not going to lie, the make up sex is pretty fantastic.

I plump one of his tartan cushions now and steel myself for the ensuing conversation. To give Bailey credit, he's made a real effort to get to know my foster family, in an attempt to 'bring us closer together' as he put it. But as I explained to him: 'They're not like your family, Bailey, they're toxic and I don't feel the need to get closer to them. In fact, it's better for my mental health if I stay the hell away.' But he insisted we make an effort for Christmas. So here I am.

Bailey frowns at the laptop, waiting for the connection to kick in, and I note he's wearing the new Christmas jumper that I gave him yesterday. As soon as I saw it, I had to buy it. It's red and has four ridiculous festive dogs across the front with 'Merry Woofmas' above their heads. He loved it on sight. In fact, he got a bit misty-eyed, hugged me tightly, and said, 'It's the best Christmas jumper ever.' So I'm feeling pretty chuffed with myself.

We just have to get through this Zoom call, and then we'll head to Waverley. Andrea and Kirk are meeting us there, and we're all travelling together to Kingussie, where Allan will pick us up from the station. I can't wait.

The screen springs into life, and my stomach tightens. Here we go. Violet appears, her kohl-rimmed eyes glaring at us like she's got better things to do. She and I gaze at each other awkwardly. There's no sign of the mother and father yet. They probably forgot.

'Morning, Violet!' chirps Bailey.

'Morning,' I say a lot less chirpily.

She nods at us.

'How are you?' Bailey asks.

Violet sniffs. 'I've been better.'

'Oh, what's up?'

I elbow Bailey in the side. Yikes, if he asks her that, we'll be here for hours.

My foster sister's mouth turns downwards. 'Not that you really care, but I hate my job, and I've just been ditched by one of my good friends for a goth muso.'

'Oh, sorry to hear that.'

'Yeah. He's not even that famous, and it won't last, I bet you.' Violet folds her arms and pouts moodily. Bailey tuts sympathetically while I stay quiet.

'What kind of music do you like?' she suddenly asks him.

'Uh, Christmas carols?'

Violet's eyes narrow, as if he's taking the piss. Unfortunately, he's really not. Bailey loves Christmas carols.

The other half of the screen flickers, and my foster parents' faces appear.

'Morning. We did say ten, didn't we?' I remark. Now it's Bailey's turn to elbow me.

The mother is fumbling in her handbag and doesn't reply, but the father gives a gruff 'Mornin'' on their behalf.

The mother sits upright and lights a fag, drawing in deeply and blowing out a plume of smoke towards the webcam. For a moment, they're both enveloped in nicotine fog.

'I thought you gave those up!' I say sharply.

'I'm trying, ain't I?' she whines. 'It's difficult.'

Bailey clears his throat. 'So what are your plans for Christmas?'

The father shrugs. 'The usual. Drive up to stay with Vi and head out to the local pub for a feed—that's if my leg holds out.'

'What's wrong with your leg?' I ask, resisting the urge to

roll my eyes. There's always something wrong with him.

'I've got a pain in it. I think it might be serious.'

'Shouldn't you go to the doctor?' asks Bailey.

But he just cackles and gestures to the bottle of Jack Daniel's beside him. 'Got all the medicinal help I need right here, son.'

'Time to go unfortunately,' I say hurriedly to get off the subject of his drinking. 'We're heading up north to Ballindalloch, and we still have to pack.'

'Lucky for some,' grumbles Violet.

'Already? We just got on,' says the mother. 'I was up early, specially to do my hair.' Her hair looks like a bird's nest that's been pulled through a bramble bush, so I highly doubt it.

'We might come and visit in the New Year,' says Bailey before I can stop him.

The mother grins, baring her stained brown teeth. 'Luvverly. I've got a bunch of DIY jobs that need doing, and you look like the handyman type.'

I see Bailey's eyebrows raise slightly on the screen, and I wince, thinking, *Not if I can help it.*

'I might not be around by New Year,' says the father morosely.

'Well, bye. And merry Christmas, everyone,' I say, leaning over to end the call.

Violet's already gone, and my foster parents wave half-heartedly through another plume of smoke emitted from the mother's cigarette. I heave a sigh of relief. Thank God that's over with. Nothing really changes with them, but we made an effort at least.

Bailey gives me a hug and rubs my back. He knows how much talking to them stresses me out. 'That wasn't so bad. I really think the mother likes me, and Violet was even quite friendly this time.'

'As friendly as a bulldog,' I mutter.

But I don't have time to dwell on the family encounter. We're too busy packing and wrapping last-minute Christmas presents. Before I zip the suitcase, I double-check to make sure our costumes are definitely in there. This is going to be fun!

Later that day

'Are you OK with that one, or do you want another go?' Kirk asks. He's manning my iPhone, which has been set up on a tripod in Bailey's bedroom.

Bailey and I are dressed as elves—the full shebang: shiny green satin elf costumes with black belts and gold buttons, matching felt hats, and long pointy shoes. We thought it would be funny if we recorded a silly elf dance for TikTok and showed it to the kids on the big screen later on. I'm not expecting much response from the general public, but it will be fun to hear Susie and Sasha screaming in excitement when they see us up there on the telly.

Bailey looks at me. 'I think one more go. OK, Holly?'

'Sure,' I say breathlessly. 'Third time lucky.'

Kirk sets the cheesy music going, and we start the dance. Bailey choreographed it. It's pretty silly, but I'm having fun anyway until he drops down on one knee. I stop mid-hip hula with my arms in the air. Is he improvising? Then he pulls a ring box out of his satin pants pocket and flips it open. Inside is a sparkling diamond ring.

'Holly Driver, I love you. Will you marry me?' Bailey's smiling so hard, and his cheeks are flushed with excitement.

What the hell? We didn't rehearse this! We have talked about it, and he knows I want it. But his timing!

'Yes,' I say, grinning like a fool. 'I love you too. Yes yes *yes*!'

Bailey slides the ring on my finger and stands. Then he picks me up in a big hug and twirls me around and around until we're both giggling madly and my elf feet are flying up in the air. He manages to give the camera a thumbs up on the final twirl.

Kirk cuts the video and smiles at us. 'Congratulations, guys!'

'Were you in on this?' I ask accusingly as he shakes Bailey's hand and gives me a kiss on the cheek.

'Of course.' He looks at my phone on the tripod. 'So shall I publish it?'

I half groan and half laugh. Do I really want our proposal to be splattered all over TikTok? I haven't got a huge number of followers, but the ones I do have are all supportive of my posts. That's why I agreed to do the elf dance when Bailey suggested it.

'All right, go on then.'

After Kirk hands me back my phone and makes himself scarce to give us some privacy, I see he's captioned the video 'WATCH THROUGH TO THE END WOOP!' and added a bunch of Christmas-related hashtags. It's already got 600 views, twelve likes, and a comment from one of my TikTok friends:

Congratulations. You guys are so cute!!!

Bailey nestles his chin on my shoulder and peers at the screen. 'Yeah, we really are.'

'You're a stinker,' I say, but I can't stop smiling and looking at the ring on my finger.

He chuckles, knowing well enough by now that my jibes mean the exact opposite where he's concerned. 'Shall we go and play it on the telly for everyone now? This is going to be classic.'

I glance at the TikTok, and it's still clocking up a crazy number of views and likes. Suddenly, the numbers jump exponentially, like it's got a life of its own. My heart starts pounding in my chest. I've seen this before. 'Oh my god, Bailey,' I say faintly. 'We're going viral!'

He takes my phone, turns me to face him, and wraps his arms around me protectively; and I know it's going to be different this time. No more running away, no more hiding who I am. Strangers can comment if they want; they might like us or hate us, or think I need a haircut—I don't care. I'm going to marry the man I love, and that's all that matters.

'Looks like Unjolly Holly got her happy ending,' I say with a laugh, gazing up at Bailey.

'Aye,' he replies smiling, leaning down to kiss me. 'It's a Christmas miracle.'

~THE END~

Keep Reading

If you liked *The Holly Project*,
read on for the first chapter of *My Double Life*.

Struggling to make ends meet, Emma McTavish takes on a
side-gig as a life model to earn some extra cash.
Knowing her straitlaced realtor boyfriend won't approve,
she keeps it quiet.

But her spur-of-the-moment decision starts making life
complicated. Suddenly she's juggling her job, her boyfriend,
her sexy new flatmate, *and* posing nude for a bunch of
strangers. Then, one night, she accidentally overhears a
conversation that changes everything.

As her life begins to fall apart in spectacular fashion, Emma
realises that giving her alter ego the reins isn't such a bad
idea. Actually, it could be the perfect way to get out of
the mess she's in.

Available on Amazon and Kindle Unlimited

My Double Life – Chapter One

CALLUM'S WEST END FLAT

✳

'It's not exactly *sexy*, is it?' Callum surveys my comfortable beige bra with an expression of distaste.

I shrug. 'At least it's clean.'

Honestly, every time we're about to have sex lately, the subject of my underwear comes up. The man has lingerie on the brain. I'm not sure what the big deal is. My M&S bra is a functional piece of clothing. It keeps certain pieces of flesh where they're supposed to be. Besides, he usually whips it off me in five seconds flat, so why spend hard-earned money on expensive wisps of lace that aren't even supportive?

'Mmm, you smell nice, like the tropics,' he murmurs, sniffing at my neck. He slips a hand round to deftly unhook my offensive bra.

'It's Jamaican Delight body wash,' I say. (It was on sale at Superdrug. I thought it sounded exotic.)

A ridiculous urge comes over me to start singing 'I've Got a Lovely Bunch of Coconuts', but Callum isn't amused by silly stuff. Instead, I bite my lip and concentrate on undoing the lower buttons of his blue-and-white pinstripe shirt and unzipping his grey suit trousers. It's Tuesday night, and he has to work later. He hates the rigmarole of getting dressed after sex, hence why he's fully clothed and why I have my blouse unbuttoned, bra flapping loose, and skirt hiked up. Now with a quick series of hand movements, Callum edges my matching beige knickers down around my thighs, then checks his Apple Watch to make sure we're on schedule. Apparently, there's a new contract he wants to look over tonight . . .

Callum actually does have a great body, when he deigns to take his clothes off (that's usually reserved for Friday nights or the weekend, when he has more free time).

The fact that he's seriously built didn't escape my notice when I first met him two years ago. I'd taken a half-day off work to view some flats through Duncan Stratt, a letting and estate agency in the New Town. While I was waiting for the letting agent to appear, I noted the pop-up calendar of Antarctica on his desk—the only thing of interest in his sterile office. Idly, I picked it up. For September, there was a photo of a fluffy baby penguin alongside a dizzying number of scrawled appointment times.

Intrigued, I wondered, *Has he been there? Or does he want to go?* I assumed a man who had an Antarctica desk calendar must be an outdoorsy, adventurer type. Since I'd been expecting someone who was a bit rough around the edges, I was taken aback when he strolled in. Callum Stewart was the most well-groomed man I'd ever seen. He had short black hair gelled back hard into place, a clean-shaven jaw, salon-shaped eyebrows, and ice-blue eyes. He was wearing a black three-piece designer suit that fit him to perfection—not a speck of lint dared cling to it.

My face must've reflected my surprise because he flicked his eyes to mine, then to the calendar, and with remarkable perceptiveness, he said, 'A Secret Santa present. Too cold for me. I prefer going somewhere warm for my holidays.'

Callum took off his suit jacket, then unbuttoned and rolled up his white shirtsleeves. My eyes flicked over his lightly tanned, supremely muscular forearms, which suggested that he not only worked out but had also just returned from a holiday. He looked like the type of guy who'd stay in a five-star resort in the Bahamas.

His handsome, put-together presence was slightly intimidating, which irked me, so I replaced the calendar and couldn't resist a flippant, 'It looks like you have been somewhere warm recently, nice tan.'

The instant the words were out of my mouth I realised it was too familiar and flushed bright red. But Callum seemed amused, and I caught him giving me a once-over as he sat down. I was wearing my typical work outfit—cream silk blouse, grey pencil skirt, natural sheer stockings, and black three-inch heels. My long brown wavy hair was tied back in a bun, and I had on my black thick-rimmed, oversized glasses, several coats of long-lash mascara, and a generous slick of pink lipstick. I call it my 'sexy librarian' look, and since I am actually a librarian, I figure I can get away with it.

Leaning back in his chair, Callum fingered his blue silk tie and considered me carefully. Then he said in a low voice, with his eyes fixed on mine, 'So are you ready to see some flats, Ms McTavish?' I swear to God my insides turned to jelly.

Anyway, that was our first meeting. When I look back on it now, it seems strange to me that he didn't even say hello or introduce himself. It was like he didn't feel the need to bother with niceties.

I force my attention back to the present, and Callum is on top of me. He thrusts a few times, grunts, and then it's over. Sex with Callum is, shall we say, *perfunctory*. He thinks foreplay is a waste of time. The most I can hope for is the odd ear nibble or breast grope. That's when he's feeling particularly amorous. He mostly just wants to do the deed and then move on with whatever tasks are next on his list.

He calls it 'pipe maintenance'.

The weird thing is it didn't start out like that. We used to have sex that lasted a normal length of time. But he started increasing the 'pipe maintenance' sex until it's pretty much become our go-to.

The first time it happened, about six months into our relationship, I was shocked beyond belief and seriously thought about dumping him right then and there. But Callum explained that it was just to save time and that he had some work to finish and that he still really liked me.

So I've gotten used to it. It's just the way he is. And all men have their foibles, don't they? Things you have to put up with?

Our sex life does tend to ramp up when we go away on weekend minibreaks. However, our last minibreak in the Lake District was a case of him thrusting three times in the morning and three times in the evening, which admittedly did leave us plenty of time for sightseeing.

Callum sighs and rolls off me, and I almost say sarcastically, 'Was it good for you?' But I just rehook my bra, button my blouse, pull up my knickers, lower my skirt, and head out to the kitchen, throwing 'Cup of tea?' over my shoulder as I go. Leaving him to sort himself out is my way of getting back at him.

Why should I have to rebutton and zip up everything I

undid exactly—I glance at my phone—four minutes ago?

Of all the rooms in Callum's three-bedroom flat, I love the kitchen the most. It's huge. All high-end appliances and black marble countertops. He has an Italian coffee maker, a blender with ten settings, and three ovens (not that he ever cooks anything). I could honestly just hang out here the whole time. One of the advantages of him moving into sales is that he has the pick of the bunch when it comes to lettings—he doesn't have to wait until something's advertised, which is why he moves flats every six months. He likes to live in different streets of central Edinburgh so he can provide 'local knowledge' for his clients.

His previous New Town flat had a Jacuzzi bathtub and a rooftop garden with views out to the Firth of Forth. I shed a few quiet tears when he handed in his notice. This current flat is in the West End in Palmerston Place, and he's been here five months. I know he's keeping an ear to the ground, so I've been using the blender as much as possible to make all kinds of smoothies before he leaves.

Maybe next time I'll suggest we have sex in here, I muse, flicking the switch on the gleaming chrome Dualit kettle. Callum could position himself behind me and thrust three times while I steep the tea. Then we can sip Earl Grey, and he can read the *Financial Times* and tell me what the share market's doing while I inspect my nails. He won't even need to see my underwear.

The scary thing is Callum might actually get on board with it. I glance at his fridge, where a weekly planner is held up by a couple of Duncan Stratt magnets. For Tuesday, September 9, he's written 'Emma' in the 7 p.m. slot—fitting me neatly in between 'meeting with Simon' at 6 p.m. and 'work on Harpington contract' at 8 p.m. Yes, he's all about efficiency.

I know I'm making Callum out to be a nightmare boyfriend, and you're probably thinking I'm a shallow bitch for going out with him only because he has a nice body and a shiny kitchen. There's much more to our relationship than that, of course. We actually have quite a bit in common.

For starters, we're both only children, and we both adore Tesco sultana scones. We also like going for runs together on the weekend. Well, we start out together. He's much fitter than me, so I usually lag fifteen minutes behind and turn up red-faced and puffing. But still, it's a shared activity. Callum is also really good company when he's relaxed and not absorbed in his work, and we watch a lot of Netflix.

We get along famously with each other's families too. Callum's parents live in Jersey. I speak to his mum and dad on the phone when they ring, and they seem to like me. I also met his cousin, Robert (or Rabbie, as he told me to call him), who lives in Skye. We went up there one bank holiday weekend for a minibreak. Rabbie's unmarried and a farmer. He and I got on the whisky, and it was a brilliant laugh. It's a shame we haven't seen him since. Callum doesn't seem keen to go there again even though I've suggested it a few times.

He much prefers to visit my mum in Fort William. She adores him and always brings out the best china like he's royalty or something. She cooks his steak just the way he likes it too—so rare it's mooing—and fusses over him like he's the son she never had. Callum laps it up.

So you see, everything is all fine with us—it really is. I've just been dissatisfied with the physical side of our relationship lately. More so than usual. I just wish he'd make an effort to please me. Yes, I've tried talking to him. To be honest, things did improve after I did. He really seemed to get what I was saying about the sexual response cycle and listened intently when I was going on about the plateau phase. Well, he nodded a lot at least, and his eyes didn't glaze over. After *the talk,* he was very attentive, and we spent a few amazing evenings together. He didn't even open the *Financial Times.*

But it hasn't lasted. Callum's lapsed back into three-thrust Freddie, and I know if I say anything again, I'm going to come across as a nag.

The unfortunate part is that I've started looking at other guys on the street and wondering why I'm putting up with it. I'm thirty-two and in my prime, for God's sake!

The kettle finishes boiling, and I pour scalding water into our mugs and dunk the Earl Grey tea bags distractedly. Besides, what if we get married and he's so focused on his career that I don't have a baby until I'm forty? Is his swiftness in the sack going to be a problem? If he barely manages to get me aroused, then surely it's going to make it ten times harder to get pregnant at that age.

OK, he's never actually mentioned anything remotely along the lines of marriage or kids, so I could be completely barking up the wrong tree . . . Maybe I need to find out subtly before I get too ahead of myself.

Callum wanders into the kitchen, raking his hair back into place and tucking in his business shirt. He opens the fridge and peers in optimistically. He does it every time he comes into the kitchen. I can tell you exactly what's in there: a bottle of ketchup, a mouldy lemon, a bottle of milk, half a bottle of flat champagne, and a wilted bunch of lettuce.

I'm not sure what he's expecting to see if he doesn't go food shopping. One of these days, I'm going to smuggle in a chocolate gâteau just to see the look on his face when he opens the fridge.

'Can you hand me the milk, please,' I say. He gives me

the bottle, and I sniff it gingerly. It smells freshish. He leans against the counter, then flicks open today's copy of the *Financial Times* and starts reading an article. I bring over his tea and lean next to him, blowing on my own to cool it down.

'Callum?'

'Hmm?'

'Er . . . Do you want kids?' Whoops, so much for subtle. Callum jerks like I've prodded him with a red-hot poker.

'What?'

'Kids. Do you want them?' I repeat slowly.

'Uh, I haven't really thought about it.' He avoids my gaze and sips his tea.

'Well, you're thirty-six. Surely it's crossed your mind?'

'Perhaps. But not in a fully formed "I definitely want this" kind of way.'

'Oh.'

'Why? Don't tell me you're getting all clucky.' He sounds slightly panicked.

'Not especially.'

Callum puffs out a breath and smiles at me. 'We're all good, aren't we? No need to rush into things. We're just barely getting started.'

'We've been together two years,' I state pointedly. 'Shouldn't we be discussing things like this?'

He turns me around to face him and puts his hands on my shoulders. He's wearing his realtor expression, and I know what's coming.

'Having a baby isn't the answer to your problems, Em. You need to sort out your flat situation.'

'It's not my fault the landlord keeps putting up the rent!'

The shitty bastard's done it twice now. It's the main reason why I haven't been splashing out on sexy lingerie and why I've started buying discounted microwave meals. I'm always complaining to Callum, but he says the landlord is within his rights to do it as long as he gives me three months' notice.

He soothes me now with, 'I'll find you a cheaper flat. Just tell me where you want to live.'

'I want to stay where I am,' I state firmly. 'I just can't afford it.'

Callum drops his hands from my shoulders and returns to his newspaper. After a pause, he suggests casually, 'Why don't you get a flatmate?'

'A flatmate?'

'Yes, you've got two bedrooms, Em. Just rent out the other one. Problem solved.'

I shake my head slowly. 'I don't want a flatmate. They'll have friends over and be using my kitchen and lounge. And they'll want to *chat*.' I shudder. 'You know what I'm like.

I'm an introvert. When I get home from work, I just want my own space—to read, watch Netflix, or think—without someone nattering in my ear. And I've got my library set up in the spare room.'

'Sorry, Em. Unless you move to a one-bedroom in a cheaper area or move in with me'—Callum shrugs his shoulders—'I don't think you've got any other choice.'

Also by Angela

You Had Me at Ice Cream

A sweet/clean, dual POV, friends-to-lovers
romantic comedy.

I'll Meet You in Florence

A spicy, opposites attract romantic comedy
set in London and Florence.

The House of Dating Disasters

An enemies to lovers romantic comedy with humorous
antics, witty banter, and spice.

My Double Life

A love triangle rom-com with shocking secrets,
hilarious mix-ups and a heartfelt romance.

Travel & Mayhem

A funny, friends to lovers rom-com with a
slow burn romance, and spice.

All books available on Amazon and Kindle Unlimited

Acknowledgements

Thank you for reading *The Holly Project*. I hope you enjoyed it! If so, I'd be thrilled if you left a review or star rating on Amazon and/or Goodreads.

As always, I'm grateful for having a team of people to help me on the publishing journey. Thank you to my beta readers, Belle Henderson and Lauryn Lambert, for your insightful and honest feedback. Also, thanks to Peachy Yap for her impeccable copy-editing and to My Lan Khuc Valle for her lovely Christmassy cover art!

To receive alerts on upcoming releases,
sign up to my newsletter at

➜ angelapearse.pub

About the Author

ANGELA PEARSE writes quirky romantic comedies that capture the humour of everyday life. A freelance copywriter with an MA in English, she enjoys travelling, hiking, cooking, binge-watching Netflix, and reading copious amounts of chick lit. Originally from New Zealand, Angela currently lives in Edinburgh with her partner. Visit angelapearse.pub.

www.ingramcontent.com/pod-product-compliance
Lightning Source LLC
Chambersburg PA
CBHW010743210726
48287CB00013B/2919